Keepers
of Equilibria

by Noreen Arangies

Wordweaver
PUBLISHING HOUSE

This is a work of fiction. Names, characters, businesses, places, events and incidents are either the products of the author's imagination or used in a fictitious manner.

First published in 2014

Published by
Wordweaver Publishing House
Tel: 00264-61-257071
P.O. Box 11579
Klein Windhoek
Windhoek, Namibia
wordweaver@iway.na

ISBN 978-99945-82-17-4

The Body needs the contribution of all parts to function to its full potential. Without you or me, where would the Body be?

Dedication

This book is dedicated to my husband, Jacques, who understands my wild imagination and encourages me to set it free. Thank you for never growing tired of all my questions and discussions, and for accepting my weirdness.

Acknowledgments

My sincere thanks and gratitude to my publisher, Bryony van der Merwe, and Wordweaver Publishing House for making this book a reality. Many years have passed since I last played with imaginary friends in my mother's garden, but your hard work and dedication has helped make the magic of this childhood fantasy come true.

I am also truly grateful for the support from my family and friends, and would like to extend a special thanks to my sisters Eunise van Wyk and Ursula Witbooi for their valuable input.

Dwarven Vocabulary

Ale – beer

Aye – yes

Bonny – pretty/beautiful

Boon – deal

Canna – cannot

Da – dad

Doona – do not

'em – them

Gonna – going to

Jest – joke

Ken – know/thought

Lad – young male

Lass – young female

Mayhap – maybe

Me – me/my

Nay – no/not

Nayr – never

Och – oh

On the morrow – in the morning

Ruse – trick

Tis – this/it's

Twas – was

Verra – very

Wanna – want to

Ye – you

Yer – your

Chapter 1

Captivating … that's what it was, and on a warm summer's day it seemed extra special when the first golden rays spread over the horizon to light up the valley. Sunrise was the most breathtaking theme in the forest of Equilibria.

The scent of fresh morning dew blended with the sound of laughter as three keepers frolicked in the grass near the creek. Their robust playfulness had them chuckling and tumbling to the ground.

Airon, an airling, jumped high and spun quickly. Dusty tried to grab him, but being an earthling, he could not get off the ground. Instead he blew upon the sand and a nasty dust cloud caught Airon in the face. The airling coughed and descended rapidly. Drizzle, an aqualing, was ready and before the other two could attack each other again, leapt at them and plunged their faces into a mud pool. The three looked at each other and broke out in laughter, rolling over onto the grass.

"Do you ever wish for a moment to go back in time?" Dusty asked once he had caught his breath and squirmed into a more comfortable position on his stomach.

Airon and Drizzle shared an astonished look.

"Whatever for?" asked Drizzle curiously.

"To see them in action of course," said Dusty, stroking his red mohawk thoughtfully. "Don't you wonder how cool it must have been to see the heroes of Equilibria … well … being heroes and all? I mean, we're talking about our parents! They were about eight and ten summers old when things went down, more or less the age we are now. But we do nothing except explore the forest. I wish we could have an adventure like they did."

Drizzle nodded silently in agreement, but the ever-chirpy Airon just grinned and threw his hands in the air in a mocking stance. "Duh huh, Drizzle and I are six and ten summers old. You are only five and ten summers. We still have time. Who knows, perhaps adventure will find us too."

"That's exactly my point," Dusty said, rolling his eyes in irritation. "We're nearly the same age as they were, but all we do is train, explore the forest and help out at the outpost. Nothing exciting about that."

Before Drizzle or Airon could answer, they heard a soft rustling sound. A loud sneeze broke the silence, quickly followed by another one. "Achoo, achoo."

Almost falling forward, an odd-looking creature appeared. The three keepers took in his big potbelly, long beard and braided hair, before leaping up and moving backwards. They could not take their eyes off the stranger.

"Good morning," he smiled. His green eyes twinkled and he spoke with a strange accent.

The young males were speechless. This was the funniest looking being they had ever seen. At about two feet tall, he was a giant compared to their kind. He wore a helmet with two horns sticking out, underneath of which ran two thick braids of what used to be red hair, now streaked with grey. His clothes were made from animal skin and his boots from a similar furry material. Around his waist was a belt of silver. He carried a bag and a huge axe.

"Good morning, sir," Airon finally spoke, breaking the uncomfortable silence. "I am Airon from the airling tribe. These are my two friends – Dusty of the earthlings and Drizzle, an aqualing."

"Oh my, finally I get to meet me some keepers again," said the stranger, rubbing his palms together in excitement. "'Tis been near to a quarter century since I last saw yer kind. Tell me how are Quake and Cyclone doing? Any news about that hard-headed Thekku?"

The three keepers gave each other puzzled looks. It seemed as though the stranger was familiar with some of their tribe elders. Who was this weirdo?

Submerged in thought, Drizzle silently went over the facts in his head as he stared at the imposter. *The forest they called home was named Equilibria, which meant perfect balance and harmony. It was hidden in a big mountain range, stretching across a valley. In its centre lay Mount Dashar. Equilibria was full of luscious plants, insects and animals of every kind. Its inhabitants flourished amongst the crystal clear pools and rivers. Shaped in all kinds of sizes and colours, the flowers appeared magical, creating a breathtaking kaleidoscope to look at. But Equilibria was a secret. Very few outsiders knew about it or the keepers.*

Related to the natural elements, the keepers came from six tribes, each of which had a duty. The earthlings were responsible for the earth, the aqualings looked after all water needs. The four winds of the sky were commanded by the airlings. The woodlings concerned themselves with the big forest trees, leaving the plantlings to care for the plants, flowers and the grass. The zoionlings were the animal protectors responsible for the animal kingdom. All tribes lived together in perfect harmony. No, Drizzle shook his head, *according to his account there were no giants around. So, where did this male come from and how did he know the elders? Most importantly, what was he doing there?*

Drizzle heard the dwarf sneeze and complain about the grass being responsible for his uncomfortable reaction, as he rubbed his already very red nose.

"Who are you, sir, and what brings you to Equilibria?" Dusty asked.

"Aye, I ken ye would ask me that and that ye doona ken who I am," he said, scratching his beard. Then he bowed low. "I am

Boforic, a law keeper from the race of the mountain dwarves. Tis a great pleasure to meet ye."

"A law keeper in our lands?" exclaimed Airon, unable to help himself. "What brings you here?"

"Ye lads doona ken the story 'bout the great treaty of twenty years ago?" asked Boforic.

The three males looked nervously at each other and then all answered in a chorus, "No."

The dwarf's eyes grew big in surprise. "How old are ye lads?"

"We are five and ten, and six and ten summers past, sir," answered Airon.

"Aye, I see yer perhaps too young to ken," said Boforic thoughtfully. "I thought yer elders told the old tales to their young ones. Och! Tis sad they did nay tell ye about it."

Boforic looked around for the path that led to the old meeting place. Surely he could not be lost. It had only been about twenty years since he had last set foot in this forest. He wanted to ask the three young lads, but they did not even know the story of the great battle and the treaty that followed it. This was a problem. He would have to rebuke the tribe elders for not teaching their young about this. If the young do not know, they might make the same mistakes and that could not be allowed.

The red-head tilted his head slightly. "Sir, are you lost? Perhaps we can help you?"

Boforic studied the young earthling called Dusty. He reminded him of Muddy, he even had the same red freckles on his face. Apart from the strange mohawk haircut, his hair was the same dark red-brown colour.

"Are ye the son of Muddy the Brave? Ye look just like him." If he was, then perhaps not all was lost. Mayhap he could still get to the great council on time and read to them from the sealed scroll.

"I am, sir. How do you know my father?" Dusty asked, baffled.

"Och, so many questions!" said the dwarf, momentarily annoyed. "Who does nay ken Muddy the Brave? Aye, that lad – and all the Light Bearers – had courage and saved the forest. Everybody ken that they are the heroes of Equilibria."

"You knew our fathers? We've always heard them called heroes, but we don't know what they did. There are tales, but who knows how much of it is true?" he said, deliberately avoiding the eyes of the dwarf and pretending to study his nails.

Boforic could not believe his ears. He was talking to the sons of heroes, who did not understand why their fathers were called heroes in the first place. Frowning, he looked the three males over again and decided that they were indeed the sons of Aire, Muddy and Raine. The resemblance between Drizzle and his father was unmistakable. It was only the bright-eyed Airon who seemed very unlike his father. The lad had a welcoming face like sunrise over the sea. Sure, he had Aire's clear blue eyes, but his playful smile and deep-set dimples were not the likeness of his serious father.

"Aye, I ken yer da's," said Boforic, scratching his beard, "but I canna understand that ye doona ken the history of the tribes."

Then his eyes lit up and he cocked an eyebrow.

"Ye are jesting with me, aye? If ye five or six and ten summers past, ye nay too young to ken about the treaty… yer da's would nayr have failed such an important instruction."

All three lads stared back at him with guilt written all over their faces, but it was only the airling who donned a silly grin.

Boforic's laughter rumbled in his chest and he shook his head in disbelief. He rubbed tears from his eyes as he retrieved a leather pouch from his bag.

"Och aye, I suppose ye right to nay trust a stranger in yer lands," he said, opening the pouch and retrieving a scroll from it. "Here is proof that I speak the truth."

"Is this the treaty that was signed?" asked Dusty excitedly.

"Och nay, lad. Tis proof of the treaty. The treaty is in a secret place."

Airon stepped forward and took a peek. His eyes scanned over the words as he mumbled, "*Keepers of Equilibria, you are an ancient, noble race. For thousands of years your kind has taken care of this beautiful forest. Although the responsibility of this task is not an easy one... blah blah blah.* Ok, he seems to be more friend than foe. We can trust him.*"

"My apologies, sir," said Airon, looking at the dwarf, "you discovered our trick. Please understand that we cannot trust strangers."

"Aye, ye lads are smart. Twas a good ruse ye played on me. Now tell me, are ye responsible for outposts?"

Drizzle cleared his throat as if to gain courage. "We are going to find out soon enough, sir. With the next full moon, we will gather with our parents and the elders, where they will repeat the history of our race and also explain the choices we have. We get to choose to remain with them and build the village, or start a new outpost. It's still one more rising before the great gathering."

Boforic had an idea. He could bargain with the lads to join him on his journey to the old meeting place. This way they would not know that he was lost. His ego could not allow him such shame. Besides, he could give them some schooling along the way and mayhap it would turn out to be a pleasant journey. A big smile crossed the dwarf's face.

"Well lads, do ye wanna join an old dwarf on his journey to the Sacred Cave? I can give ye a boon for it."

"What's a boon, sir?" asked Airon, frowning.

"A boon, lad, is when ye do something for me and in return I do something for ye."

Airon shared a glance with his companions and could tell that they all shared the same excitement about travelling with the dwarf. It would be more fun than exploring the forest.

"We accept your boon, sir," Airon spoke on their behalf. "It'll be an honour to walk with a law keeper and learn more about the treaty. Perhaps you can tell us about the Light Bearers and their quests."

"Good choice, lads," said Boforic, relieved. "Let's make haste then. Tis a journey, after all."

So, the males and the old law keeper set off north, in the direction of the Sacred Cave. The old meeting place was hidden inside the mountain in the centre of the forest.

They walked for a while through the long grass. Boforic seemed to have become accustomed to the grass, because he no longer sneezed.

"I'm happy to see the tribes still getting along after all these years," he commented. "I remember the dark time when twas nay so."

They waited in anticipation for the dwarf to start his version of the legend, curiosity tugging at them. They wanted to know exactly what had happened. Until now, they knew only the outlines – their parents had never wanted to brag about the part they had played, and therefore the details were sketchy. They had heard tales and rumours about the battle, but nothing more. Excited, they hoped that Boforic would tell them everything, especially about the role of the Light Bearers.

Boforic remained silent while they ascended higher through a rocky slope. He thought back to the once different Equilibria and the dark time that had plagued it; a time he hoped never to witness again. But before he began his story, he needed to establish just how much his audience already knew.

Chapter 2

"Tell me lads, do ye ken how old yer kind can get and when ye can choose a lifemate?"

The young males seemed puzzled by his enquiry, but Airon enthusiastically clarified a few facts. "I believe so, sir. Our kind can grow up to fifty and one hundred summers old. There are claims that some have reached two hundred summers." He whispered the last part as though revealing it in confidence. "What about your kind, sir? How old do you get?"

The dwarf did not even spare him a glance as he dryly stated, "Och, 'bout three hundred summers. Who kens, mayhap even four hundred summers."

"How old are you then, sir?" asked Dusty.

Boforic considered the red-head for a brief moment and then pointed his nose into the air, taking a deep breath. "Wanna shame an old dwarf, laddie? Ask yer question later again, mayhap then I would tell ye. Now, Bright Eyes, what were ye saying 'bout maturity again?"

Airon frowned at the pet name the dwarf had just given him, and tried to get his mind around it. He was not sure if he mentioned anything about the maturity of keepers, but before long his cheerful smile returned. He wiggled his eyebrows playfully and continued.

"Our kind are considered mature at eight and ten summers past and we can choose a lifemate each year at the feast of Solace. This means that in two summers both Drizzle and I can find a mate if we want to." He pushed out his chest and beamed at the statement, before rubbing Dusty's mohawk. "Unfortunately our friend here will have to wait still another summer before he can make a lovely female smile."

"Who said I want a lifemate?" asked Dusty, slapping Airon's hand away. "Maybe I just want to be a warrior. Besides, who needs the feast of Solace to make a female smile?"

"Well, I'm sure your recklessness will forge a great friendship with all the others set on becoming warriors. I can think of one dark-haired, dangerous female in particular," Airon teased.

Dusty's eyes flew to Airon's and his skin began to shimmer. "Shut your big mouth, Airon," he said angrily, "and while you're at it, wipe that grin off your face too. My life, my choices."

As if to further aggravate his earthling friend, Airon shrugged nonchalantly and wriggled his fingers in front of him. "Ooh, scared of the little Raven, are you?" he asked.

"Yer friend?" Boforic inquired, keeping a steady pace.

"Raven is Shadow's niece – his adopted daughter. She spends all her time with her pet hawk. Word is that her battle tactics are unmatched and she never misses a target," Airon replied softly, as if in fear that she might hear him.

Boforic nodded in agreement. He remembered Shadow, the mysterious animal protector. "Ye still have nay answered me question," the dwarf countered.

"Huh-uh, not exactly a friend, but we are brethren, I suppose. She is Shadow's daughter, that makes her a southern outpost keeper and Dusty's most feared opponent," the airling answered with a big smile, as he dodged a mud ball.

Boforic found it amusing that serious Aire had sired such a cheerful young male, while charming Raine had a solemn offspring. *It must be nature's way to pay back the fathers for the mischief of their youth*, he mused. He didn't know what to make of the red-head yet, except that he could sense an adventurous spirit in him.

"Tell me lads, why are ye nay of the same age?"

"That sir, was the next part I was getting to," said Airon, his eyes sparkling like sapphires, "before this red-head here shocked us all with his cutting words. Anyway, like I said, we get to claim our mates, get mated with binding vows and then we have to wait for two summers before we may ask permission from the council to have a youngling. Dusty's father met his mother one summer after our parents mated. And that's why he is a summer younger than us."

"Why do ye have to get permission from the council to have young?" asked Boforic curiously, scratching his beard.

Airon opened his mouth to answer, but it was Dusty who announced seriously, "Only two young per couple is allowed. The elders say it is to keep balance in the forest. Keepers must at all times be balanced in equal numbers amongst the different tribes. This ensures that we are able to fulfill our duties and maintain the peaceful existence of our race. Over-population could result in division and the forest can only carry a certain number of living beings. It's part of our duty as keepers to assist in the cycles of nature. So, young are only allowed if the numbers of the race are low. If not, then a couple must wait until the time is right."

"In our case, the great battle reduced the numbers of our race and our parents didn't have to wait long for permission," added Airon.

"Aye, of course, it all makes sense," said Boforic. "Perfect balance in the forest of balance. Ye lads all seem to ken the workings of yer race well enough."

His gaze shifted to Drizzle as he spoke, but the young male did not seem the least bit intimidated under this direct inspection. Boforic smiled at his quiet confidence and shifted his gaze back to the horizon.

"Ye wanna ken more of what happened, aye?" Boforic finally asked.

"Yes, sir," the three replied swiftly, their heads bobbing up and down in eagerness.

"Let me start at the beginning then," said the dwarf.

The forest was as serene and beautiful as ever. Right in the centre, at the foot of Mount Dakar, was the lovely city of Par – the stronghold of the keepers. It was a safe haven for all the tribes, who lived together as equals.

Eons before, the elders had decided to expand the kingdom and protect the borders of Equilibria. They chose to do this by forming outpost teams. Each team consisted of a representative from every tribe who trained together and, when ready, were sent to their chosen outpost, where they lived and functioned as one body. A team commander was chosen who, when summoned, would attend council meetings with the elders to discuss any progress or difficulties at their outposts. Insects were used to summon the outpost commanders as they were superb messengers. Although many different types of insects were used for this job, bees were the favourite because they were swift and reliable.

Once the team had settled and their area was flourishing, team members were allowed to travel from time to time. The feast of Solace took place after every harvest, and during this festival unmated keepers were allowed to choose a lifemate. Once coupled, the new pair would rejoin the outpost team, in time get permission to have a youngling and complete the cycle of their lives. There were outposts in the northern, southern, western and eastern regions.

The south was considered the untamed region of the forest, mainly because the mountains stretched thin there and this allowed more foreign species to gain entrance. It was also situated the furthest from Par, and therefore the keepers of this area were accustomed to living in isolation. This area was home to many different animals, as the river flowing from north formed a small pond that was nicely tucked away in a clearing. A few streams flowing from it formed a path that led back into the main river. Beautiful flowers grew nearby some bee colonies. Further south were rocky highlands with small caves, which could be used as shelter, but their main dwellings were built at the bottom of large oak trees. Secured and camouflaged, their small, almost invisible kind easily hid there.

Aire, Raine and Muddy were busy tending to the forest when suddenly Maple, a woodling appeared.

"Have you seen Lilly?" she asked, doing her best to look worried. "She's been missing for hours."

Muddy peeked enquiringly at Maple from under his brow. He knew that Lilly had gone off with Shadow earlier and had a feeling that Maple was up to something. It was normal for her to stir up trouble. Glancing across at Aire and Raine, he could tell that they had a similar suspicion.

Maple, with a crop of brown hair, was shorter than most keepers. She jiggled her long pointy ears when the males ignored her. She was aggravated at their disinterest and lifted her perfectly arched eyebrows, which complimented her big brown, intelligent eyes. Then she tilted her oval-shaped face and rested her hands on her hips. As she did so, the complex design of light golden bands, which covered the length of her forearms, shone brightly.

Raine lowered his head and Muddy turned his in the opposite direction, quickly smothering a smile. Their indifference was obvious and a pink blush spread over Maple. *How dare they ignore me*, she thought, gritting her teeth. She lifted her pointy nose a little higher and pouted her lips even more. It only added to her mischievous look. When she swung around in frustration, her skirt of orange leaves lifted a little higher from its normal position just above her knees. She stormed away and then stopped in her tracks, as if she had just remembered something. Slowly she placed one knee-high boot made from soft wood bark, behind the other and turned around again.

"Why do we always have to look for Lilly? Some of the flowers are so full of nectar that they look sad. She needs to call the bees. Where did she disappear to this time?"

Muddy shrugged his shoulders and continued to dig his fingers deeper into the earth, as he tilled it. Muddy was a practical keeper. He did not like to wear fancy stones, such as diamonds and emeralds, like his fellow earthlings did. Instead, he wore a tunic and pants woven from plant fibres and mineral threads. His eyes shone like two polished amber stones. Concentrating, his nose got all wrinkly and the light freckles that covered his nose and cheeks formed a pattern which looked like skipping stones.

He focused for a while on an area and then asked Raine to wet the ground. Raine rubbed his hands and water droplets fell as required.

Aire, the commander of the outpost team, was blowing grass seeds into the air.

"You know Aire, you are too easy on Lilly," Maple continued to complain. "She gets away with everything. I think it's because she is so pretty that you allow her carelessness, while the rest of us must work hard all day long."

"Maple, are you fishing for a compliment?" asked Aire, lifting his brow. "You know very well that all female keepers are beautiful. It doesn't matter which tribe you belong to." Aire stretched his arms lazily above his head and yawned. "Anyway, we are keepers not slaves. We are all entitled to a bit of fun. If Lilly and Shadow want to explore, they have every right to do so, just like we do."

Maple pulled a face and clenched her fists into balls. Raine sensed that Maple was about to explode and decided to put an end to her fury.

"Maple, please quit your venomous attack," he said smoothly. "Give us your magical smile, won't you? You have an incredibly

13

beautiful smile. It's such a waste when you say angry words instead of stealing our hearts."

Raine, the handsome aqualing, was a real charmer. He was confident and always knew what to say to the females. Maple looked at his perfect chiseled face and wondered how the other males could live with Raine's arrogance. With spiky silver hair and deep blue eyes, he was magnificent and he knew it. His broad shoulders and muscled body made him look like a great sculpture. Greyish skin and clothes that shimmered like a mirror ensured that you could see your own reflection on him.

Maple got annoyed just looking at his perfection and decided to put him in his place. She rolled her eyes and crossed her arms. "Oh Raine, you're such a flirt! Your compliments won't make me forget that you're letting Lilly get away with this."

Just then, Lilly and Shadow came rushing across the field with haunted looks on their faces.

"Well, well, guess who decided to join us," Maple muttered.

Lilly, an ethereal plantling, looked baffled and although her lips moved, no words came out.

"Brethren, you will never believe what I've just heard," said Shadow. "I heard from one of the parrots near the stream, that a basket of nuts has disappeared from a storehouse in Par."

A swift and doubtful "What?" response came from everyone.

"But that's impossible," said Aire, shifting uncomfortably. "Who would take a basket from storage?"

"Someone probably just misplaced it," suggested Raine, looking as confused as everyone else.

Keepers shared everything amongst the different tribes, including food. In Par, all lived together in close proximity in the trees and everyone had a specific duty. The elders were responsible for all the important decisions and the governing of the city. The wellbeing of the tribes rested upon the shoulders of the older females whose duties were to take care of the dwellings, make clothes and care for the younglings. The growth and prosperity of the tribes was assigned to the older males, whose duties included the goodwill amongst the tribes, building new shelters and the harvesting of food. The outpost teams of young matured keepers were responsible for protection and tending to the needs of the forest.

"What a strange occurrence," said Muddy, unable to stop himself from thinking aloud. "Do you think that somebody would have taken it for themselves?"

"I don't know," admitted Aire, rubbing his chin. "Something like this has never happened before. It's the strangest thing and I'm sure the elders will investigate and get to the bottom of this. I'll enquire about this matter at the next meeting. Hopefully it's just a mistake."

As much as he tried to make it sound like a trivial incident, the whole thing bothered Aire. Other than the fact that it had never happened before, it was highly unlikely that anyone else but a keeper could have taken or misplaced the nuts. The storage chambers were well-guarded and great care was taken with their contents. No animal could enter without a guard being aware. Besides, the zoionlings had a pact with the animals. They protected them and in return, animals stayed clear from the homes and belongings of all keepers. It simply didn't make sense and Aire's gut told him that trouble was brewing.

As he turned to walk away, he felt eyes watching him. He angled his face slightly and caught the dark gaze of Shadow. *Of course, he'd make the same assumption*, Aire realised. Aire knew that his words may have placed the others at ease, but it did not have the same effect on the animal protector. Shadow lifted an eyebrow at him and his gesture was confirmation that he did not believe that the missing basket was unintentional or taken by an animal. Aire turned his head more, staring straight into the raven eyes of Shadow. It was a silent acknowledgement between the two of them.

Chapter 3

"I'm thirsty and hungry. Can't we rest for a while?" Airon asked, rubbing his stomach with a pained expression.

It was nearly midday and the four of them had been walking at a slow, steady pace for hours.

"Aye, ye lads are strong, but even the strong must rest," said the dwarf, after a moments consideration. "Let's sit and enjoy some nourishment."

Airon's mouth quirked slightly upwards. The dwarf was obviously a warrior of old, but he was also a very dramatic one. And of course, very slow. They could have reached their destination much quicker, but the big dwarf moved at the speed of … an image of an oversized rodent popped into his head and a silly grin spread over Airon's face. Well, at least the dwarf was interesting and informative.

They sat under a rocky ledge and Boforic dug into his bag. He took out a wooden plate, and filled it with delicious fruits and some dried meat. Then he retrieved a goblet into which he poured liquid from his waterskin. He passed it to Dusty. He licked his cracked lips, as he gestured with his other hand to the plate of food in front of them.

Dusty took a sip of the foreign brew and turned a strange dark brown colour before he spat it out. "Phew, what on earth is that? It tastes like poison!"

Boforic snickered at the blunt outspokenness of the earthling. Then he took a sip and wiped his knuckles across his mouth. "Tis ale, laddie, and very good ale at that. It keeps up the strength in warriors like me."

Dusty was sure that they would die if they drank the strange liquid. Not to mention that the dwarf also had meat on the plate. Keepers lived off plants and food from the earth, never eating the flesh of animals. He decided to rescue them from the unthinkable fate.

"No offence, sir, but I think it's best if we stick to our own diet, although we will gladly share your fruit. I can add some mushrooms, and Airon and Drizzle can also share something."

Drizzle took a large leaf, rubbed his hands together. Water fell from his hands and filled the leaf.

Airon whistled a soft tune, mimicking the sound of the wind singing through the leaves of trees. Not long afterwards, a few bees flew to them, carrying a big piece of honeycomb. He thanked them politely as he took the honeycomb. Then he broke off a piece for each of them.

"A feast!" Boforic exclaimed, holding his goblet high. "Let us eat and gather our strength."

There, in the shadow of the ledge, they enjoyed their meal and afterwards Boforic cleaned his cutlery and packed everything into his bag again. Then he lay on his back, twisting a few strands of his long beard between his fingers. The young males looked at each other and their expressions gave away their mischievous thoughts. They were trying very hard not to laugh out loud, because their new friend looked hilarious with his big tummy pointing upwards. It had the likings of a nice bouncing surface. The dwarf must have realised that he was the cause of amusement and promptly wiggled himself upright.

"Why do young lads like ye travel alone?" Boforic asked. "Where are yer parents?"

Dusty licked the last of the sweet honey from his fingers. "We're young male keepers, sir. We have seen enough summers already and are almost considered mature."

"Grown-up, bah!" said Airon, waving his hand in an argumentative gesture. "It's more like we're old enough to work, train and get to know the forest, but not old enough to have a mate."

"You can't be serious," asked Dusty, appalled. "You really want a mate? Sure, they are pretty to look at, but I don't want one now! Some of them cry and others argue all the time."

"Well, I want one and I don't care what you have to say about it," said Airon with a wide grin.

Dusty shook his head in disgust. "Think carefully friend. We have to find adventure first."

Drizzle kept silent through this banter. Boforic frowned and his scrutinising stare rested on the young aqualing.

"Ye have the image of yer da Raine, but ye sure doona act like him. Why is that lad?"

What an unexpected question, Drizzle thought. Aloud he answered, "They say I have the likeness of my father, but the character of my mother, Dew."

Drizzle had turquoise eyes like water pools. He was quiet and, unlike his father Raine, did not like to stand out. For this reason, he wore purple and blue colours, like his mother. It drew less attention and allowed him to blend in easily amongst the other aqualings.

Boforic studied him a little longer and recognition dawned on him. How silly of him. How could he forget? Typical of Raine's style, the aqualing had drawn the attention of every keeper in Par when he claimed Dew as his mate. Who would have thought that the charmer Raine could be charmed? The dwarf smiled to himself.

"Aye, Dew it was indeed. I can see her in yer eyes and yer gentle nature. Her wit and bravery defeated even the strongest of warriors."

Did he just give me a compliment? Drizzle wondered. Both Airon and Dusty now looked at him intensely. He was immediately uncomfortable. How did he become the topic of discussion? No, he did not like to be the focal point, and he decided to change the subject.

"Sir, how is it that you know so much about our parents and elders?"

Drizzle was pleased when he saw his two friends turning their heads to the dwarf, focusing their questioning eyes on him. Deep down, he felt like he had just won a battle and he struggled to hide a pleased smirk.

For a moment, Boforic was bemused and he raised an eyebrow at Drizzle. *Clever lad*, he thought. He wiggled his back and got as comfortable as possible against the hard surface. Then he smiled, revealing his broken teeth.

"Aye, as a law keeper, I get to travel to lands and visit all the races. It's part of me job to ken 'em all and understand their workings better. Tis way I can either defend or rebuke them if justice is called for. So, ye ken, when the Ancient One summons the law keepers, we have to give an account of what we've seen and what we ken 'bout the races."

Airon's eyes grew big and then he asked enthusiastically, "How many races are there?"

"Och, let's see ... Tis ye keepers in tis forest, we dwarves in the northern mountains, Fey beyond the mountains to the south and Elves over the mountains to the east."

"Wow, I never knew there were so many races," Airon replied absentmindedly.

"Nay laddie, there are even more, but these are the ones whom I visit."

Airon opened his mouth to speak again, but Boforic cut him off with a wave of his hand, while he wiggled his eyebrows. "Mayhap I will tell ye 'bout the races on another journey, aye? All ye need to ken is that tis dwarf was visiting with yer race in Par, at the time that the division and rebellion were brewing."

"Son of Raine," continued Boforic, looking intently at Drizzle, "I was at the feast of Solace when yer da claimed his bonny mate. I also attended the ceremony of their binding vows."

Then he shifted his gaze to Airon. "Aye, I was also at the council meeting when the division began and twas there that I met yer da, Aire. He invited me to his outpost, where I stayed for a night. So ye see lads, I ken yer da's. I also visited again with them, when the treaty was signed. Tis how I ken what happened during the dark time."

Respect … that is what Boforic saw in the eyes that now watched him so closely. Their eyes shining like the jewels in the mountains. For a moment, he felt uncomfortable under their direct gazes. For young keepers, these lads sure had an intimidating presence.

Silence followed his previous chatter and he filled his lungs with the clear air of the forest as the sounds of it calmed his senses to a point of complete relaxation. Once again, Boforic realised that he loved the peace in this forest. He heard the cry of an eagle far away, and then the soft voice of Drizzle brought him back to reality.

"What happened next?"

He tugged on his beard in thought as he tried to remember what he had last told the young males. "Where were we? Ah, the stolen goods! Let me continue."

The old dwarf got a dreamy look in his eyes as he resumed the tale. He told them that two days had passed, but still the keepers could not get any closer to the truth. They did not find the basket of nuts or any evidence of the remains of it. This caused suspicion and distrust amongst the tribes. There were whispers amongst the keepers and they began to spend more time with their own tribes and less with the others. It was a bad thing as the first signs of division set in and as time would show them, it only got worse. The council decided to call a meeting to discuss the issue.

Chapter 4

The great hall filled up quickly with all the outpost commanders. Aire played with the goblet in his hand, twisting it around slowly before taking a sip. The honey bush tea tasted better than what he was used to.

He kept his gaze low as he studied his fellow outpost commanders, also quenching their thirst. Soon they would be called into the Sacred Chamber to attend the meeting. His warrior instincts were on high alert as he sensed the tension and general animosity amongst them. He regretted that he had not brought two of his team members along, as most of the other commanders had. Aire could not explain it, but he felt threatened and decided to stay as unnoticed as possible until he had more clarity about the situation.

"They live like Kings and Queens, I tell you," he heard one of the commanders say. His eyes followed the voice and rested upon Willow, the woodling commander from the western outpost. He heard the group of keepers around him agree in low tones and one remarked about the quality of the tea and the fine garments that everyone in Par wore.

Troubling, thought Aire.

A guard announced that it was time for the meeting and they all entered the tunnel that led to the cave's entrance inside the mountain. As they proceeded, Aire heard more murmuring and whispers. It was clear that there were grievances about the lavish way in which the keepers in Par lived.

Once seated, Tsunami, the forceful elder of the aqualings, welcomed them and he introduced a dwarf named Boforic. The dwarf was a law keeper and was doing his rounds amongst the different races. He sat in a big custom-made chair next to Ivy, the elder of the plantlings. Boforic was in deep conversation with her, but lifted his head, grinned at everyone and signalled that they should continue.

Once Tsunami held everyone's attention, a shocking introduction followed. "As you are aware, there have been some unfortunate happenings in Par. A basket of nuts went missing two days ago. We have also now learned that more disappearances have occurred … apples and precious material, to be exact."

The voice of Soil, an earthling commander from the western outpost, broke through the murmuring.

"And what have you done about it?" he asked accusingly.

The authoritative voice of Griffin moved unhindered through the chamber and he drew the attention of all as he spoke.

"Day and night the tribe elders have tried to solve the mystery, but to no avail. We have, at this very moment, scouts about and designated keepers involved in the investigation," he informed them, as his eagle eyes transformed into narrow slits.

There was a sudden clang as Soil slammed his goblet down on the table and laughed out loud. Griffin lifted an eyebrow at his display and Aire, sitting a few places to his left, could almost swear that he heard him roar.

"Yet still no thief, and in the meantime we can't help but wonder who or shall I say, from which tribe, the culprit comes," Soil challenged, lifting his arms in a dramatic display.

A few gasps went up and then he continued, "Why do you all sound so offended? This's exactly what everyone is wondering. It's what is whispered in the shadows."

Quake, elder of the earthlings, slammed his fist on the table and his diamond-coloured eyes grew dark as he looked at Soil.

"Soil, your displays and utterances are disrespectful to this council. You will immediately correct your behaviour."

Soil slowly rose from his chair and looked at the elder with a rebellious spark in his eye. "I speak the truth and you know it."

The air in the chamber suddenly grew very cold and a layer of ice formed on the walls. The ground shook and the sound of thunder rolled through the air, lightning bolts crashing above. At the same moment, the sound of rumbling water formed in the back of the chamber. Aire held onto his chair for safety.

"Och no, laddies," came the voice of the dwarf above the noise. "Come now, yer all grown, aren't ye? Calm down, lest ye bring down these rocks on our heads. Ye canna solve all problems with a fight, now can ye? Tis entertaining, but nay fun."

At his rebuke, the elders calmed and the chamber grew silent.

The dwarf kissed Ivy's delicate hand and added, "Och, lads always like to show off in front of a bonny lass, aye? Please forgive 'em."

Regardless of the death grip that choked his heart just a few moments ago, Aire found himself smiling at the dwarf. He liked him. Boforic looked amused as his eyes drifted over them and then with a nod of his head, he signalled again for them to continue.

"Have you considered that if one tribe accuses another, the tribes may move against each other?" spoke Ivy. "If rumors are about, the situation is already dangerous. Brethren; it could lead to war amongst the tribes and as you just saw, this could have deadly repercussions."

Drake, the zoionling commander from the east, spoke up and asked what would happen to the commanders if the outpost teams broke up. Many other commanders had the same concern. Aire felt his jaw muscles constricting and noticed that he had clenched his hands into fists. He was shocked and disappointed in his fellow brethren, they did not seem concerned by the threat of a war.

Keepers were an ancient race who had always dedicated their lives in service to each other and the forest. Never before had individual positions been of any significance. Their purpose was to guide, teach and protect. Everything was done for the benefit of the whole body and not for personal gain or admiration.

"Shouldn't we be more concerned about the threat of war than our positions?" Aire heard himself ask.

Immediately he could sense irritation in the many eyes pinned on him. Swiftly he felt the Sacred Chamber constrict. Griffin was the only one who nodded slowly in agreement, but the rest looked at him as though he was an enemy.

Dimly he heard the gruff voice of Thekku. "Without leadership there will be chaos."

All the other voices roared in agreement.

"I agree with Aire," said Griffin. "He has a point. How can you keep your positions as commanders if your team members disintegrate?"

Soil rose from his chair. "Well then, so be it," he exclaimed. "Perhaps it'll be better if we each lead and command our own kind. As it looks to us, it is beneficial to be in charge over a large group, now isn't it?" To add emphasis he waved his arms around the chamber and added, "With such fineries, you're very comfortable, aren't you?"

"Don't be ridiculous, Soil. These fineries are for the benefit of all keepers," Griffin replied.

"No, we don't think so," argued Willow, also standing. "It's you who live in Par who are clothed in soft garments. You eat and drink the best and live in luxury. We don't have any of this at the outposts."

Another argument erupted between Bushy, the plantling commander, and Gravel, another earthling.

"Quiet!" Aire heard the thunderous shout of his own tribe elder, Cyclone. Cyclone's reputation for being unpredictable preceded him, but at that moment the charged atmosphere was not defused by his command. Many commanders were standing and voices grew loud as accusations were thrown back and forth.

Aire was struck with disbelief. He suddenly realised that their attitudes were making the threat worse. It seemed to him that their true intention was power. To top it all, Drake had alliances in Willow and Soil who supported his claim to remain in power. Added to this, Soil's suggestion that each tribe should command their own chilled Aire to the bone. Disunity was fast becoming a reality. And in the midst of it, a power struggle loomed. Aire wondered how these normally sane commanders had become so selfish. His eyes scanned over the elders. They acted no better. There was no point in looking to them for leadership.

He felt eyes on him and when he looked up, the piercing eyes of Boforic met his own. It seemed as though the dwarf had taken an interest in him, because he moved closer.

Aire briefly noticed Soil and others storming out of the chamber and then Boforic spoke against his ear.

"Come laddie, tis best if we get out of here now. These foolish lads mayhap just really bring down these rocks on our heads. On the morrow the sun will rise again."

Aire realised that there was no reason for him to stay in Par and planned to return to the southern outpost the following morning. Boforic, who was headed in the same direction, en-route to the Fey in the far south, offered to accompany him.

Upon Aire's return to the southern outpost, with the strange guest from the northern mountains, he did not say much about his trip. Regardless of the growing concern, he avoided all questions about the meeting altogether.

Luckily Boforic proved to be an intriguing and entertaining distraction. He spent the remainder of the day and night with them and they enjoyed a small feast together. He told them tales of his many travels and their social interactions seemed to give him much pleasure.

Chapter 5

Maple was sitting lazily on a tree branch swinging her legs and twisting a small twig in her mouth. Squinting, she studied Lilly and a wicked smile tugged at her lips. Lovely Lilly was singing and jumping from flower to flower when Maple spoke in a defiant manner, disdain dripping from her words.

"Lilly, word is that the plantlings are the ones who took the nuts and hid them, so that they could eat them alone and not share with the rest of the tribes."

Lilly nearly missed a step and stared at Maple with big eyes. "Impossible! That is not true," she blurted out. "How can you say such a thing? We plantlings would never do such a selfish thing."

Lilly with her deep green eyes looked like she'd just seen an evil wood nymph. Her normally ethereal features and high cheekbones did not lessen the stunned look on her face. Her full red lips were trembling and her long yellow hair, spun like gold, fluttered in the wind. The deep purple gown made of flowers that flowed down to her ankles, gave her a dramatic appearance. Although a fine cloak of small silver flowers was draped over her shoulders, she trembled uncontrollably. A tear slipped over her pale cheek. She sat down on a large yellow rose and hid between the flower petals, crying softly.

Maple smirked devilishly and continued to play with the twig in her mouth. Suddenly a whirlwind swept up from the ground and it blew dust and leaves onto Maple. She nearly fell off the branch as Aire appeared in front of her with his arms crossed and his face looking as hard as stone. He was furious. Lightning sparks flew off him.

"Maple," he thundered, "if you can't respect your other team members, then you should consider joining another team. I will not tolerate any kind of evil. Jealousy, rudeness and insults certainly constitute as evil in my opinion. We need one another. You are either for this team and its members or you are not. So make your choice."

Maple was stunned at the frankness of her commander and her face turned red as she stumbled over her words. "I ... I'm not jealous. I simply said what I've heard."

"And you find it acceptable to share such hurtful things with Lilly, our own plantling? Or did you intend to hurt her? Is that why you said it?"

The rest of the team members gathered around, all shocked to see Aire so angry. He was a very capable commander but normally even-tempered. This was the first time that a team member had been given an ultimatum and they wondered why. Everyone knew that Maple could be a handful, but her antics did not normally qualify as great offences.

They all focused on Aire, their proud commander with the strong muscled build. Tall, with pale skin that shone radiantly and pearl white hair that reached his shoulders, he looked like the ever-in-charge male. His clothes were white and shiny, but being angered he appeared almost see-through. Aire was impressive to behold and nobody envied Maple at that moment.

Aire took a deep breath. The council meeting had been disappointing, and he felt guilty that he had not yet informed his team about what had happened there. Through Maple's actions, he suddenly realised how fragile the relationships between the different tribes were at the moment. The slightest tremor and his own group could fall apart. It would take strong leadership to get them through this troubled time as one unit.

Aire knew that the inevitable was coming – the possibility of war. If they did not find a way to restore the peace, all would be lost.

Suddenly the solution became clear to him. If the elders couldn't keep the peace between the different tribes, Aire would do the unthinkable … he would form a bond amongst his team that would be stronger than the bonds amongst tribe members. Their isolation as a group was a benefit and it drew them closer to each other. Maybe, just maybe, it might work. It was completely against the laws, of course, but Aire felt in his heart that this was the right course of action.

Although his resolve was clear, Aire was insecure about his own skills as a leader. Would he be able to forge a bond amongst his team strong enough so that they would not hesitate to go against their own tribes if the time called for it? Was he capable of guiding them through the dark times ahead?

Still being as coiled as a snake and ready to strike at any moment, Aire turned and looked upon his chosen warriors. Together they will have the unthinkable task of defying tribal law, destroying the darkness and restoring peace.

With flashing eyes, his gaze momentary stunned them witless. Perhaps it was because he didn't normally use his striking gaze on them. And then his voice rumbled through their haze.

"Listen carefully. Although each of us has different functions, together we form a whole. We are one unit, with one purpose and, as one, we take care of one another and our duties. No one is better than another. We might be from different tribes and we might have different tasks, but we are all keepers. We need each other to survive.

"I am aware of a separation growing amongst the tribes, but in this team it'll never be tolerated. Today, I give each of you a choice. Stay and be part of this team or leave. If you choose to stay, your life will be pledged to the lives of your team members, no matter what happens amongst our tribes. Your word will be your honour."

Aire looked at the shocked faces in front of him. He knew that he asked much. But the way was still clear in his mind – if a small group, united as one, could withstand the evil, there was hope.

Maple lowered her eyes and said softly, "I'm sorry. It was wrong of me to do that."

"You should apologise to Lilly, not me. But I am awaiting your answer. This is a serious offence and in this team, not allowed. Choose now."

Maple's eyes grew big and her lips trembled as she looked at Aire. "I choose to stay and be part of this team. This is where I belong."

"Good," said Aire.

Then he turned and his questioning gaze rested upon the rest of the team. "What about you?" he asked.

One by one, heads slowly nodded in the circle they had formed around Aire.

"Thank you for your precious gift of trust. I believe this is the only way," he said earnestly. "Then we shall form an unbreakable union."

Maple slowly moved closer to Lilly. She fiddled with her hands as she stopped in front of the plantling and softly said, "I'm sorry Lilly. It was a mean thing to say."

"I forgive you, Maple," said Lilly, giving her a hug.

When Aire spoke again, his voice was filled with emotion. "Just as Equilibria needs light, we need light amongst our tribes. We cannot allow darkness to destroy our world. We will act as the light for the tribes during these dark times. We will call ourselves the Light Bearers, because darkness will have no place among us. I will give each of us a marking of light and this will be the symbol that binds us together."

The admirable glances of his team members warmed his heart as he spoke.

"You don't know this yet, but more things have been stolen and the elders cannot get the growing division under control. I fear that we may be facing a tribal war. If we form this bond, we will be the hope of our tribes. However, you need to understand that once you've pledged yourself, there will be no going back. Your first and foremost obligation will be to the Light Bearers and not to your elemental tribe."

A few gasps went up, as the group realised the enormity of their decision.

"Let me get this straight," asked Raine frowning. "You mean to say that I would have to turn my back on an aqualing for any of you?"

"Unfortunately, yes. There's no other way. If it'll give you any consolation, consider the fact that the keepers around you have been closer to you than any sibling could have been."

Raine's handsome face looked pained, but Aire's words made perfect sense. As an orphan, he never had the privilege of growing up in a family, but neither had the rest of his team members. Orphaned or not, they had all been taken at a young age to be trained together.

It did not take them long to understand what pledging would mean and everyone solemnly agreed.

Aire paused. His eyes dark and serious, but a smile was visible at the corner of his lips. "Let me direct you in your pledge and lead you in the ceremony that will bind us."

Aire was the first to step forward and make his pledge. He crossed his right arm over his chest and rested his palm flat on his heart. Similar to the vows of the lifemate bonding, he boldly spoke the words: *I pledge my allegiance, my protection and my life to the Light Bearers. I choose to be an instrument of light and not one of darkness. As one, we will fight evil and bring justice. From this moment forth I am one with you as you are one with me, bound by honour, for all time."*

Aire held his hand over his left inner wrist and a small spark of lightning jumped from his hand onto his skin, forming a glowing mark made of light, in the shape of a sun. It was a circle and had six rays that ran outwards from it. Six rays – one for each tribe member. The circle represented their union, while the rays characterised their individuality and the light that would shine from the Light Bearers.

One by one each keeper stepped forward and pledged their allegiance. Aire held his hand over each one's left wrist, etching the symbol into their skin.

Finally they all held hands and Aire joined them to close the circle. They bowed together low before one another, the gesture indicating humble service to each other. They all uttered the words, "For light and honour," and it was done. The pact was formed.

They knew from that moment forth, they would always stand together, no matter what. Even if it meant dying for each other or facing rejection from their own tribes. There could be no division among them, only respect, honour and friendship.

Muddy stared at his glowing mark in admiration. "This is rather cool. Anyway, I've never quite fitted in amongst my tribe members. Almost every earthling I know is concerned with jewels on their garments. It is unpractical and annoying. None of you ever asked me why I don't have all the pretty adornments, but they have always judged me." As an afterthought, he added jokingly, "Besides, guess who's got the coolest decoration now. We all outrank their bogus niceties. This is real … a sun shining on us." His grin was so big it engulfed his face. Everyone laughed at Muddy's humour.

"Our markings are glowing and noticeable," said Shadow. "What will other keepers think and what should we tell them if they ask us about it?"

Shadow was an animal protector and a born defender. The zoionlings were all warriors and each possessed the skill to communicate with animals. They all had a special pet, which was always close by. It was their duty to defend all animals against invasions from foreign species. They were trained in battle and were very intimidating. Shadow had a lean muscular body with olive skin.

His face was attractive with a square jaw and high cheekbones. The muscles in his arms were well-defined. His thick blue-black hair fell over his shoulders and his eyes were as dark as a raven's. He wore a long cloak with a hood made from black and blue feathers, mimicking the feathers of his pet bird, Argon. Under his cloak, he wore a black leather waistcoat and pants with soft leather boots. From his belt hung daggers. On his back, he carried a quiver with arrows and his bow was never out of reach. Shadow was a stealth master and could sneak in and out of places unnoticed. Bearing a glowing mark obviously did not sit well with him.

"Are you afraid that the marking will draw too much attention?" asked Aire.

"Yes," Shadow replied boldly.

"You can hide it by willing it away. It'll disappear for a while, but as soon as you allow your feelings to get the better of you, it'll return. Perhaps it's not such a bad idea to hide the mark for now. At least until we know where we stand with the elders and the tribes."

"Oh no!" Muddy answered quickly, pinning Shadow with playful eyes. "Now mister hide and seek, look what you've done. What's the point of having a shiny sun if I cannot show it off?"

Shadow grinned and bowed low with his hand on his heart. "My apologies, brethren. I didn't know that a shiny sun could influence your dislike towards shiny stuff."

Aire smiled and wondered how Muddy and Shadow could always bring joy to any situation. They were a good combination.

"We need to make plans. I don't want any of you to be part of a battle if I can help it," he said. "For the time being, our main aim is to collect information. Then we can form a strategy to destroy the threat of war."

"Is this our first quest?" Shadow asked. "To act as spies?"

"Spoken like a true warrior. Yes, it is." Aire quirked a grin and mischief played in his blue eyes. "Remember Shadow, no fighting. I only want information."

"Understood …," Shadow answered with a smile, lifting two palms up in defence.

Silence fell over the group.

In an instant, their carefree lives were gone, suddenly replaced by dark seriousness. The task weighed heavily on their shoulders and by all that was sacred they hoped that they would succeed. The symbol on their wrists would always remind them of their unity and purpose. They were no longer ordinary keepers; they were now Light Bearers.

Chapter 6

The sun was setting in the west when the party of four finally crossed the steep rocky slopes and entered the lower valley. It had been a long day, but the young males were happy about everything they had learned so far. Boforic was very pleased that no one had discovered that he had forgotten the way to the Sacred Cave.

"How old are you, Boforic?" Dusty asked again, peering up from under his very long eyelashes.

Boforic smiled. The lad had just called him Boforic and not sir. This probably meant that he was now considered a friend. "Och, again laddie? Ye nay gonna give in are ye?"

A resounding "No," followed.

"Why don't you want to tell us? What's the big deal about your age? We already know that you're a law keeper," Airon said earnestly.

"If I tell ye how old I am, ye might consider me too old to be yer companion, aye." Boforic announced, marching steadily as he wiped the sweat from his brow.

"I don't think that would be possible. We have been travelling together for the entire day. So you are already our companion," Drizzle reasoned.

Boforic frowned at the lad. *The son of Raine is a keeper of little words, but his mind works. He will probably make a fine strategist*, he thought. "If ye put it that way lad, I suppose yer right. Boforic, the mountain dwarf is one hundred and seventy years old. That means lads, I have seen many summers pass."

"Well, slap me silly," Airon proclaimed in sheer joy. "I've got a friend that old. Take that! To all the older keepers, who treat us like younglings."

Ah, there it is. Boforic mused. He was considered a friend now. The confirmation made his chest feel awkwardly tight, like a high-strung note, but it left him with a warm feeling in his belly.

Clear night skies approached rapidly with the scent of sweet bushes and grass welcoming it. Airon cheerfully pointed them in the direction of a small cave that would serve as their shelter for the night. After collecting wood, Dusty started a fire and everyone gathered around it. They shared a meal of wild berries and figs, and Drizzle made them delicious honey bush tea. Boforic took out a piece of sticky sap plant from his bag and then stuck it onto a twig. He held the twig over the fire until the plant became gooey. After some time, he took three more twigs and rolled some of the gooey stuff onto them into small balls. He gave each of the males a ball on a stick and simply said, "Enjoy." Without hesitation, they ate it and they were pleased with the sweet, sticky treat.

The fire was warm and inviting, and they shared many laughs. Curious eyes of small wild animals came to investigate ever so often and the crickets were happy to sing them a song. Up in the sky, thousands of shining stars were spread out like diamonds on a black velvet cloth. It was a good ending to a good day.

A few hours into the night, the young males got comfortable on a small rock, while Boforic rested against the cave wall. The dwarf straightened himself and removed his furry boots. His round feet were covered with thick woolen socks and both his big toes poked out of the holes in them. Seemingly unaware of the amusement that he was causing, he got comfortable and uttered, "Ah."

The cave grew silent as they stared into the dancing flames. The young males were still thinking about the pledge and the quest that had set their fathers apart as heroes and Boforic could see the keen interest and excitement in their eyes. Although he was tired, he decided to entertain them for a little while longer.

Boforic cleared his throat, "I should tell ye the beginnings of their quests, aye?"

Three heads nodded in agreement, sparkling eyes looking up at him. The old dwarf stretched out his arms, cracked his knuckles and took them back in time again.

After the ceremony, the Light Bearers enjoyed a meal together. Aire found it the appropriate moment to discuss the way forward. It was time to start gathering information. Five pairs of eyes followed him as he paced up and down in front of the rock that his keepers were seated on.

"The feast of Solace is approaching," he finally said. "Raine, you shall go to Par under the disguise of finding a lifemate, where you must gather as much information as possible. What stirs in the north and what is happening in Par? See if you can find out the plans of the elders."

Raine nearly fell from the rock and the rest of the team laughed out loud. Everyone knew how much Raine liked the attention of the females and that he would not be happy with the attention of only one.

Raine struggled to form words, but finally said, "I … I'm not ready to find a lifemate."

Aire smiled. "I did not say go and find one, I said use it as a disguise. Everyone's well aware that you'll not settle easily and no one will find it unusual if you leave without one. Just stay for a few days and then excuse yourself. They're aware that our outpost is not the easiest to tend to and that you can't stay away for too long."

Looking visibly relieved, Raine agreed to the terms.

Aire then turned his attention to Maple. "Maple, you will be our eyes and ears in the east, where I suspect trouble will come from under the leadership of Drake. He has formed alliances and is a threat."

"Drake the dominating! You can't be serious? We've never liked each other. He'll find my travels there suspicious."

"I know," said Aire, crossing his arms. "That's why you're the perfect challenge for Drake. You're our special potion, Maple. Drake won't be able to handle someone as feisty as you. Just use your famous dramatics and all should be well. Tell them you need to find out what trees would grow best with our old Oak. They have some similar areas to ours and shouldn't think too much of it. Spend a few days with them and see if you can find out anything about their plans."

A devilish smile formed around Maple's mouth. "I must admit, I'm up for the challenge. It would please me to upset Drake. I am at your service, chief."

Everyone laughed. Then Aire turned to the animal protector. "Shadow, I want you to fly west and spy on the keepers there. Use your stealth – no one needs to be aware of your presence. Learn as much as you can and return swiftly. It shouldn't be too big a problem for you and your pet. When you sit on the back of Argon it's impossible to see you. It still amazes me how the two of you can blend together so perfectly."

Shadow's pet was a fierce-looking hawk-eagle with complex pattern designs on his feathers of blue, white and black. He had a crest of long feathers on his head that formed a crown when raised. Argon had piercing eyes that shone golden. Centred in the middle of his fiery eyes, two irises the colour of darkness gave him a vicious appearance. His legs were striped and looked as though they were clothed in feathery boots. His yellow talons were large and powerful, and prey did not escape them. His tail was long and marked with black bands and his wings were broad and rounded in flight. As it was between all zoionlings and their pets, the pets normally chose their masters at a young age. In the same manner, young Argon had chosen Shadow. They could not just sense each other, but could also read each other's emotions and had the ability to communicate telepathically. Zoionlings shared this unique connection with all animals, but the bond between master and pet was much stronger. Shadow and Argon formed a dangerous combination, a force to be reckoned with. Without a word, Shadow lifted his right hand to his brow, saluted Aire and gave him a casual bow.

"You have three days to gather information. The rest of us will remain here and continue as if nothing is amiss. The ground is still moist so Raine's absence should not have a big influence for now. Maple, you and Shadow must secure your perimeters before you go."

Aire looked at his three spies and wondered if he made the right choices. In his mind, he went over their special qualities again. Shadow was his unseen force, Maple was his weapon to create havoc and Raine could extract any information easily from the ladies. He had definitely chosen the right spies. The first part of their quest should not be too difficult. Dangerous yes, but hopefully they would be able to pull this off without any problems.

Aire expected an eerie silence from his team, but instead they all seemed excited. He had every bit of faith in his Light Bearers. They would never betray each other; neither would they fail in their duty, no matter how difficult it was.

It was time. In the old ancient warriors greeting, he grabbed Raine's two forearms and looked him straight in the eyes. Then he gave him a sincere nod and released him. He did the same to Shadow, but when he came to fiery Maple, he smiled and gave her a hug instead.

They all cried out, "Light and honour," one last time and with the greeting, "Stay safe, Light Bearers!" he sent them on their way.

Shadow whistled and Argon flew down out of nowhere. Shadow jumped on his back and they took off with grace, flying high within seconds. Raine showed off his perfect teeth with one of his best smiles and jumped into the creek. The current would rapidly lead him to his destination. Maple kissed her fingers; then blew the kiss towards her teammates. She spun around, hopped into the nearest oak tree, and swiftly jumped from branch to branch, quickly disappearing out of sight. With that, the three spies were gone.

Chapter 7

Maple strolled along the path to the east and sang a happy tune. She had crossed the thick, dense trees and was now moving along grassy fields. Far ahead lay the grove of ageless trees. She felt a bit lonely without any trees nearby to talk to. Eventually she decided to seek company. She found herself stopping ever so often, to speak to an insect or small animal. They did not scare her as much as bigger creatures did.

Just as she was reached the end of the field, a hand grabbed her waist. A male keeper pulled her against him and spoke into her ear, "Ha ha, look what we have here, a little woodling far away from home."

Maple screamed in fright and he immediately covered her mouth with his other hand. "No screaming. We've got enough trouble already."

Without thinking, Maple sank her teeth deep into his hand. Her capturer let out a cry. "Ouch, you little wildcat!" He threw her to the ground.

Maple couldn't breathe. Her heart was racing and blood was pounding in her ears. She lifted her head slowly and froze. Her capturer was a zoionling. Although naturally good-looking, this zoionling looked strangely neglected. His hair was long and messy with four braids on each side, a sure sign that he was a warrior. With grey eyes like a wolf's and a mouth currently curled into an alarming sneer, he reminded her of a mad beast.

Maple swallowed hard and lifted her head defiantly. "I'm not a wildcat."

Laughter rose behind her and she turned around, staring into another pair of animal eyes, only these were more catlike. *Why do all zoionlings have animal-like eyes?* she wondered.

Maple smiled at the newcomer, who looked friendlier than the first one. "Would you please inform your friend here that he forgot his manners? It's not proper to grab females like that, especially not a guest in your lands."

"You don't act like a female," said the unkempt one. "And who says these are our lands?"

Maple looked up at him and frowned as she made an impolite "Humph" sound; disregarding whatever authority he thought he had. She got up and dusted herself off.

The other one laughed again. "Let it go Fenrir. It was just a wee bite. Let's just take her to Drake. He will know what to do with her."

Fenrir furiously moved towards her again and pushed her into the direction of his friend. "You bind her then. She's got teeth as sharp as a cat."

"It's a good thing my pet is a feline then," the other one said with a grin on his face. He held out his hand to her and said, "Come, I'm Leo. Give me your hands. I don't want to fight with you. Besides, you'll only make things difficult for yourself."

Maple stared at Leo for a moment. Her heart was still racing, but her mind was focused. She knew that she had to play along, or she would get hurt. Slowly she lifted her hands. He pulled them together and fastened them with a piece of braided grass.

Acting like a helpless damsel in distress, Maple looked deep into Leo's eyes, attempting to overthrow him with her charm.

"Why are you capturing me? What have I done wrong?" she said in a sweet innocent voice. Leo watched her with an amused sparkle in his eyes and a smile on his mouth.

"Stop asking so many questions. Drake will give you the answers you seek."

"I mean you no trouble at all. I was just passing through. I wanted to gain information from the outpost team on what other trees would grow with the old oaks. Now, you drag me off like I am some kind of outlaw." She added a sniff for good measure.

Her story took him aback. She saw the confused look on his face. Hopefully he was beginning to believe in her innocence. But Leo shrugged his shoulders and moved along the path. *Oh no! It didn't work*, Maple thought in frustration, stamping her foot.

Then Fenrir said, "It'd be wise if you keep quiet woodling, until you're asked to speak." Maple gave him a dirty look and pulled a face at him. He gritted his teeth and pushed her forward. "Move," he grunted.

She knew that Drake was not a patient keeper and he would be less inclined to give her any information at all. Now was her best chance to gain knowledge. Hopefully with a little bit of urging, his friends would be more willing to share some news. She did find it strange that there were so many zoionlings and wondered where the rest of the outpost team was.

Push them harder Maple, she said to herself. "Why are there so many zoionlings here? Where's the rest of your team?"

Leo's eyes almost pleaded with her to surrender as he attempted one last time to tame her. "Woodling, you ask too many questions. You're amusing, but your disobedience will get you into trouble."

She rolled her eyes. "My name is Maple and surely my questions are not difficult. Or do you have trouble understanding me?" Maple knew that implying that they were thick in the head might be risking too much. It was a direct insult, but she had to do something.

Fenrir snapped and moved in front of her. She bumped right into a wall of hard solid muscle. Maple held her breath, her pulse flickering fast in her neck.

"Look wildcat, these lands now belong to the zoionlings and unless you want to be fed to my pet wolf, you better keep quiet," he said with conviction.

She ignored his threat. "The zoionlings? You must be mistaken. An outpost team keeps these lands."

Leo shook his head in disbelief. "You're a stubborn one, aren't you?"

Fenrir looked at her with astonishment and she noticed that his dove-grey wolf eyes were actually very intriguing. Then he said, "Implying that we are daft, huh? Take a good look at yourself before you say that to anyone again." Suddenly she didn't find his eyes so appealing anymore. They obviously thought that her persistence was senseless and that she had a nut for a brain.

She seethed in silence, and after a few more minutes they arrived at the main keep of the outpost. More zoionling warriors appeared from the dwellings at the bottom of the trees and gathered around them. A huge lump formed in Maples throat, fear crippling her. Fenrir had spoken the truth – the eastern outpost belonged to the zoionlings now and by the looks of things, she was their prisoner. What had she gotten herself into? *No! Don't let them see that you're scared. Control your fear and give your audience a show. You may be a prisoner, but not for long.*

Drake came walking towards her, with long strides. "Well, well, what do we have here? Look who came to visit. What are you doing here, Maple?" he said, tilting her chin to look at him.

Taking a huge breath, she forced a playful smile on her face. "Drake, I can't say that I'm happy to look upon your face, but since you are the only recognisable keeper around here, could you please ask your friends to let me go. I was on my way here to find out what trees we can plant with the old oaks, when these two oafs abducted me," she replied, sounding almost like an offended youngling.

Drake lifted his brow and his beautiful turquoise lizard eyes gave her a penetrating stare. Then his mouth fell in a hard line and it made him look cruel. Staring into his eyes made her uneasy and shivers ran down her spine. His fair hair was pulled back into a ponytail and decorated with a few colourful feathers. She noticed that he also wore the four warrior braids on each side of his head.

"You expect me to believe that you're here for the sake of duty? Gee! I am so impressed, " he said sarcastically.

Maple threw her bonded hands up in frustration and looked as sincere as she could. "Why else would I be here? Look, I'm tired and hungry. I've travelled far and would like to rest. I have not done anything wrong, so please release me."

Drake scratched his chin. "No."

She stared at him in disbelief. "You can't be serious. You are violating the code of the keepers."

His eyes flickered and for a moment, she thought she saw flames leaping inside of them. "Watch your words and don't tell me about codes, woodling. Where have you been? Don't you know war is at hand?"

"What on earth are you talking about?" asked Maple, astounded, "Have you gone nuts? War in Equilibria? You have time for silliness, while the rest of us work hard."

Drake grabbed her arm, a menacing grin at the corners of his mouth. "Silliness you say? Obviously Aire is playing *mister righteous* as usual. Well fiery one, you have been misinformed. The peace is broken. The tribes are now fighting for themselves. That means you, little woodling, are now my prisoner."

"Let go of me," Maple demanded.

"Or what?" he mocked, squeezing her arm tighter. "I don't think you are in a position to be giving orders."

Maple's eyes grew wide. This was not part of the plan. She was not supposed to be Drake's prisoner. "A dominating Drake I can tolerate, but cruelness does not suit your handsome face," Maple defended.

Drake blew her a mocking kiss. "Maple, Maple. Flattery is not your style."

"You're insane, Drake. Let me go. Aire will come for me and you'll die if you hurt me," she pleaded genuinely.

"I'm not scared of your airling and don't be so sure that I'll be the one dying," he said flatly.

He loosened his hold on her a little bit, as if he was going to dismiss her like a youngling. Maple could not help the fury that rose within her and she saw her opening. Without giving it a second thought, she lifted her two fists and punched Drake in the face. She caught him off-guard and his eyes widened in surprise. His hands flew up, trying to stop the blood that was now flowing from his nose. "You'll pay for this, you little minx! But not yet … you will first learn how to respect your new master."

"I will never bow to you, you brute!" Maple said, almost spitting out the words.

Drake laughed out loud. "Throw her in the dark chamber, add some rope to her ankles too and put a guard at the entrance. I'll decide later how to make her pay for her disrespect. Aire will come and look for his little woodling. I look forward to testing his strength."

He swirled around to walk away, and then he suddenly paused. "Oh, and Maple, don't forget that you and I don't like each other very much. As fascinating as you are, don't expect any favours from me. After all, you are my enemy now."

Maple's breath caught in her throat. She knew he meant every word. Her cheeks flamed with anger as two animal protectors dragged her to the entrance at the bottom of a big tree. *Indecent rogue! I will get you for this*, she vowed.

Chapter 8

Shadow hugged Argon's neck tightly as they soared higher. What a sight Equilibria was from up there. They could see the river with all its streams and pools, the entire valley and higher lands. The view was spectacular. They were nearing their destination and soon the clearing of the western keepers would be visible. Packed with high luscious trees, it would supply good cover.

After a few more minutes of enduring the wind and flying with agile speed, the clearing came into view. Shadow smiled at the sight. It was carpeted with beautiful colours. He bent down a little lower and spoke into Argon's ear as he pointed. "Over there my friend, to the left, where the silvery trees are. We'll blend in easily amongst them."

Argon shifted in mid-air and dived. He stretched out his claws and moved in a manner of attack … only it wasn't really one. It was all part of the plan. From the ground, it would look like he was nothing more than a predator going in for the kill. It was natural for birds of prey to hunt in the forest, so nobody would think anything strange of the unexpected company.

They landed on top of one of the highest trees, from where Argon could scan the area. His superb eyesight allowed him to spot a mouse a mile away, so very little went unseen. Shadow slid from Argon's back and squatted next to him on the branch they had landed on.

Finally, after a lengthy silence, Shadow whispered. "There, south-east. I can see four keepers – all woodlings. Why so many of one tribe? Where are the members from the other tribes?"

Argon blinked at his master twice and Shadow's eyes grew big in suspicion, like two deep black pools. It couldn't be possible. Had the tribes already divided?

Shadow frowned and took a good look at his surroundings, taking in everything. He noticed a patch of dead grass, some withered plants and worse, a few dying trees. The dark warrior pursed his lips as he spotted a solitary tiger in the tall grass. The carnivore seemed to be distressed for no apparent reason. Instead of its distinctive *chuff* greeting, the big cat gave a fearful growl, while it stalked up and down, thrashing its tail in agitation. Whilst he still tried to get his head around the cat's strange behavior, a fox not far from him, gave a clearly recognisable scream. The high-pitched noise was normally only reserved for the night and this particular one indicated that the animal was unhappy. Shadow's intelligent eyes quickly scanned the skies and instantly he became aware that even the flock of Blue Jays seemed noisier than usual. In fact, when he studied the rest of the rabbits, deer and the lonesome wolf in the area, all of them also showed uneasiness. Almost as if they sensed a storm approaching. This lack of balance in the forest confirmed Shadow's suspicion – the division had reached the west. But where were the caretakers of the area? Had they been driven away by the woodlings? A foreboding sensation crept over him. Shadow had to find out exactly what was going on and his gut told him that it was not good.

They sat on the branch for another hour, carefully studying the group of woodlings who were completely unaware that they were being watched. They were lying around lazily, eating and chatting. They appeared unorganised, allv talking at once and no one seemed to be in charge. Then four woodlings came from the direction of the pond and joined them. One of the woodlings was taller than the others, and he immediately took charge.

47

Ah, so he is the commander, Shadow realised. He wondered whether they came from Par or from other outpost teams. If the latter, it would mean that the other outpost teams no longer existed. Shadow looked at Argon and nodded. The keeper climbed back onto his pet's back and gestured his head towards the stream. The hawk-eagle dived and then shifted upwards again into a breathtaking display of flight. In seconds, they were high in the air again. Argon circled a few times producing a penetrating and far-carrying *keewoowee* cry. The hawk-eagle had to act normal, so that they would draw the least possible attention. It worked. Not one of the woodlings even looked in their direction.

When they reached the stream, Argon landed on a log at the edge of the bank. Shadow slid down and whistled a soft tune. Moments later, several animals approached. Cats, deer, rodents, crawling animals ... they all came and stood in front of Shadow. He looked them over, and then bowed before them. "Greetings, friends. It's an honour to meet you. We've come from the south and seek your council as to what has happened here in the west. My eyes do not betray me and what I see is not good. Can you share any information?"

A big spotted cat moved forward and communicated telepathically. *Welcome, great animal protector. We are pleased to meet you. It is true what you speak. Great sorrow has come to these lands. The team of keepers that was assigned to us has been captured by a band of woodlings. They paved a path of destruction in their quest, harming trees in the forest to make weapons – big weapons like battle-axes and hardwood hammers. We've heard them talk. Their commander is called Willow. He told his guards that they joined forces in the city of Par and moved north, but a rebel group of aqualings had already made the north their stronghold and forced the woodlings out. So they came here and overpowered our keepers. No one is taking care of our area now.*

Shadow pulled a hand through his midnight blue hair. It was worse than he expected. Aire had been right to act so soon, he thought ruefully. War was on the horizon. Suddenly it struck him that Maple might be in danger. If the aqualings had taken the north and the woodlings the west, it left zoionlings, earthlings, plantlings or airlings to form a stronghold in the east. He would have to fly that way to make sure that Maple was unharmed and not in danger.

But first, there was a task still to be done here.

"Where are the prisoners being kept?"

The big cat looked deeply into his raven eyes as he imparted the information. *In a cage downstream. It's a wooden cage, but it's locked and we could not free them. There is one guard.*

Shadow grinned at the knowledge. "We'll get them out. Was the woodling keeper also captured, or has he joined the rebel group?"

A gray rabbit hopped forward. He wiggled his nose and moved his whiskers about. *They gave him a choice to join their rebellion, but he refused, so they locked him up with the other keepers and they are not kind to him. They treat him as if he is as guilty as the rebels. It is an unstable situation.*

Shadow now fully understood the motivations behind Aire's extreme actions. The other teams would not last; they only had a duty and breakable friendships that kept them together. Only they, the Light Bearers, had a much stronger bond, formed through honour.

Shadow bowed again. "I thank you for your help, oh graceful creatures of the forest. May goodwill and protection rest upon you! Do not despair, we will fight this evil and win. We will restore balance to these lands. Go in peace now, till we meet again."

The group of animals moved off and disappeared quietly into the forest, leaving Shadow and Argon staring at each other. Their quest had become a rescue mission. They took off again, flying downstream. Argon settled on a high branch, from where they could see the cage. It dangled from a tree and a wooden latch secured the door. They studied the setting and then Shadow reached for the quiver on his back and took out an arrow. He dug into his cloak pocket, took out a small container, and then dripped a few drops of the concoction onto the point of the arrow. Raising his bow, he took aim at the guard. The arrow flew and pierced the woodling's shoulder. He cried out and fell. He was asleep before he hit the ground.

Shadow reached for another arrow and aimed. Next followed a *thump* as the arrow penetrated the latch of the cage, breaking it into pieces. The door flew open and the six keepers jumped out, landing beside the sleeping guard. They looked both confused and relieved. Shadow covered his head with his hood and Argon dropped him in front of them. Keeping his head low, he stepped forward and retrieved his arrows. Then he pulled the guard to a rock and placed his arms under his head, to make it look as though the guard had fallen asleep.

He smiled at Argon. *The sleeping mixture knocked him out cold. He won't remember a thing when he wakes*, he communicated to his feathery friend with a few blinks of his roving eyes.

The six keepers stared at him.

"Please don't kill us," cried one.

"I won't kill you. I've freed you, haven't I?" Shadow muttered dryly, keeping his gaze low. "Leave here and go to Par. You should be safe there."

The earthling stepped forward and stretched out his right hand to touch Shadow. "We thank you, sir."

Shadow jerked back. "No need to thank me. Just get out of here now. You don't have much time before the rebels return."

The keepers looked at him like he was some kind of hero. Shadow didn't feel comfortable with their admiration. He preferred being unnoticed and unseen. He mounted Argon, but before they took off, he lifted his head and said, "One more thing, your woodling keeper is not part of the rebels; so don't treat him as one. Do you understand?"

Quiet heads nodded in acknowledgment. He heard a few of them commenting on his dark, dangerous eyes and then, deciding that he'd had enough, coaxed Argon to leave. The hawk-eagle flapped his wings, raising a cloud of dust.

Shadow whispered in Argon's ear. "Thank you, trusted friend. Now get us out of here. All this attention is making me nervous. To the east!"

Chapter 9

Maple was sitting in a corner beating her fists in frustration against the wall of the tree chamber. The action wasn't comfortable, since her wrists were still tied with the braided grass rope. She heard a rustle of footsteps approaching. Two more warriors joined the guard outside. She could hear them joking and laughing. *Sure, have fun while I sit here and waste time.*

"Once we have taken control of Par, all keepers will bow to the zoionlings and we will live like kings. The ones who control Par control Equilibria! The time is drawing near, so stop complaining and get us some food," said one of the warriors.

The blood drained from Maple's face and her thoughts turned chaotic. *They are crazy. We can't allow this to happen. I need to get out of here now! Think, Maple, think!* Panic rose as she tried to come up with an escape plan. Her fists beat at the wall again and suddenly a sly smile formed as an idea came to mind. *Silly zoionlings! Did you forget that I'm a woodling? I can command wood."*

Although it was dark in the chamber, she could see well enough. On the opposite side of the chamber were a few barrels filled with honey bush tea. The smell of it was unmistakable. Maple got up slowly and hopped to them. Her inhibited mobility annoyed her and she could hear the soft gnawing of her teeth in response. For a moment she considered getting rid of the restraints around her ankles, but soon cast the idea aside – it would be safer to leave them in place for the time being, until she was sure that the guard would not check on her unexpectedly. She placed her hands against the wall of wood bark and stroked it in admiration. "Oh, beautiful wise one. A wood child needs your help. Please assist me in my hour of need. Give me wood powder to put in the drinks of those who keep me against my will. I need them to get sick, so that I have time to escape."

As she continued to stroke the wood, a fine dust rubbed into her hands. She gathered it awkwardly and poured small amounts of it into the barrel openings. The whole process took longer than preferred, because of the silly restraints. Placing her hands on the wall again, she said sincerely, "Thank you, oh great one. Your kindness will always be remembered."

Knowing that victory was close, Maple rubbed her hands on her clothes and hopped hastily back to her corner, almost losing her footing completely. Her belly made a few somersaults as her excitement grew. "Now I wait," she said, tapping one finger impatiently against her cheekbone. After a while, a zoionling appeared at the entrance. He placed a wooden plate in front of her. It had a few scraps of mushrooms and wild berries on it. Maple watched him without saying a word. He moved over to the barrels and poured some of the honey bush tea into a big pitcher. On his way out, he mumbled. "A thank you would be in order, but I suppose you woodlings don't have any manners."

Maple smiled at him and politely said, "Forgive me, I'm just terribly scared."

At first he smiled, revealing two perfect dimples, but when Maple lifted an eyebrow at his gesture, he gritted his teeth and walked out of the chamber.

Yes! Yes! Yes! Maple cried softly, suppressing the urge to shout it out loud. She sat back and enjoyed her meal. She listened to the joyful bursts of the zoionlings, their bragging and laughter, for what seemed like hours. *Not long now and you will all be crawling on the ground with stomach cramps. That will serve you right for treating me like a criminal.*

When the noise outside finally quietened down, her hand lowered to her boot and took out a small blade hidden in its collar. With haste, she cut through her restraints and popped the blade back into her boot. She rubbed her wrists a bit to elevate the discomfort she still felt at the imprint left by the rope. Moving as softly and slowly as possible, she made her way to the entrance and paused. Maple's pointy ears peaked as she listened to every sound. It was noiseless and then … there it was. She could make out the faint sounds of groaning. "Gotcha! Time to leave," she whispered under her breath.

Tilting her head around the entrance, she took a peek outside to scan the area. As expected, her guard was rolling on the ground clenching his stomach. No one else was in sight, but she would still need to be careful. After taking a step towards him, she stooped over him. Seeing him lying so helplessly, her resistance crumbled against the urge to tease him. She patted his head and smiled deviously.

"Oops, seems like you're not feeling too well. I'm so sorry. Unfortunately for you, you will start retching in the next few minutes and then you will feel very weak. Don't fear though, it will all pass soon enough, but in the meantime I'm out of here," she whispered in a low voice to him.

Then she turned on her heel and ran as quickly as she could in the direction of the grass fields. From behind her, a voice shouted. "Stop her! Stop her! The little wench is getting away."

Uh-oh! So much for making a quiet escape, she thought. *Just get to the trees, Maple.* It was late afternoon and the sun was moving over the mountain. Soon it would be dark. Zoionlings were great trackers and on top of that, they always had their pets near, which gave them an added advantage. The knowledge that they could recapture her if she was not clever drove her wild. Deep down, she knew that she would not be so lucky next time and neither would they be as merciful. The mere thought of looking into Drake's eyes again made her nauseous.

She ran as fast as her slim little legs could carry her. Once she reached the trees, she would be able to move faster. They would also give her shelter and keep her hidden. Suddenly arrows started to fly past her and Maple's blood ran cold. *Oh no!* Her illness inducing powder had obviously not affected all of the zoionlings.

A fierce battle cry echoed in her ears, and glancing over her shoulder, she saw three terrifying zoionling warriors pursuing her at a rapid speed. The light was fading fast now. Another arrow flew past her, missing her by inches. Then she heard a loud *keewoowee* cry in the air. Fear rose in her throat as she looked up and saw a dark shadow crossing over her. *By all things sacred, no! Escaping the zoionlings only to end up as food for a hawk!*

Her foot slipped and she stumbled, falling to the ground. Quickly she dragged herself up again. As she did, two talons circled her small waist and lifted her up into the air. She struggled to escape and squirmed as much as possible. No luck! The natural cage that the bird's talons formed was solid. She tried again, hitting against it with her arms, but it was useless. She was no match for the hunter.

As they flew, her capturer let out another fierce cry. Exhaustion took over and her frail body became limp. Weightless she hung in her trap. She just couldn't fight anymore. Looking down she saw the warriors in the distance staring up at her. *They certainly seem pleased, knowing that I am about to be the dinner of a fierce bird of prey.* Then she noticed that one of the zoionlings had collapsed, with an arrow sticking out of his shoulder. *Strange, where did that come from?*

They grew smaller and smaller until she could not see them anymore.

A few days ago, those same keepers would have defended her against the bird, but now they were happy to see her fall fate to such a cruel death. Of all the ways to die, this was not what she had in mind. Tears streamed down her face as she tried one last time to fight her way out. She was so scared.

"Maple, please stop moving. You're throwing us off balance," she heard a familiar voice say. She gazed up into the raven black eyes of Shadow. She had never felt more relieved or happier to see anyone.

"Shadow, thank goodness! I thought I was going to die."

Shadow hung low over Argon's back. He smiled at her, then reached down and ruffled her hair as though she was just a little youngling.

The Light Bearers came for me. They didn't let me die. Maple relaxed in the safety of Argon's talons and for the first time she felt like she was valued.

She enjoyed the wind playing through her hair and the scenery below. After a while, she looked up again and called to Shadow. He peeked over Argon's body again. "Yes?"

"Did you shoot those arrows?" she asked inquisitively.

"Not all of them," he replied.

She shook her head. "But that means that you shot at members of your own tribe … you did that for me?"

Shadow rubbed his fingers together, like he always did when he was thinking. "I suppose I did, but that's what we vowed to do for each other. We are now Light Bearers, Maple. There's no turning back."

His words hit Maple like cold water. Shadow was right. They were there for each other. She did not have to rely only on herself anymore. Before, when they had been only co-workers, she had seen her fellow teammates only as that, but now she suddenly realised the true meaning of the pledge they had made. She belonged somewhere and would gladly entrust and sacrifice her life to those who were her own.

"Let's go home, sister," she heard Shadow say.

"Yes, let's go, brother," she replied.

Argon shifted and changed direction to the south. "Take us home, Argon."

As they flew over the eastern region of Equilibria, Shadow noticed the big brown patches everywhere. *So, the eastern region of the forest is also dying*. He found it strange that both the western and eastern region were drying out and dying in only a matter of days. Shadow pondered over this strange phenomenon, but then remembered one of the old sayings: *Were evil increases, death comes swiftly*. It seemed a logical explanation. Jealousy, greed, anger and envy … these were the factors that had tipped the scale of balance in their once peaceful Equilibria. It would require repentance, forgiveness, peace and a lot of love to tip the scale back again.

Chapter 10

Raine paddled on his back as he entered the familiar city of Par. The stream had carried him faster than expected. The sun was still high as Raine lay peacefully, the water swaying gently under him as he floated through the high trees.

Keepers from every tribe were out and about. Some followed the small footpaths that connected the different dwellings of their kind. Their homes were built inside the trees. The trunks of the big trees were hollowed out with chambers and staircases connecting all through the length of each tree. Some of the trees had hidden underground chambers, neatly tucked between the thick roots. The airlings had entrances higher up in the trees, but the main doorways of all dwellings were found at the foot of the big trees, and always hidden by a trapdoor in the bark of the tree, or covered by thick grass and plants.

Raine smiled brightly as he noticed a small earthling's head stick out from beneath a pile of leaves. His eyes sparkled with mischief. More younglings of every tribe laughed and played in a small clearing between two big oak trees. They tickled each other and rolled in the grass with delight as their nursemaids cheerfully watched on. Some screeched with high-pitched giggles, while others tried to get away. The mature keepers were going about their daily chores unfazed by the noise the younglings were making. He could see some females carrying baskets of food, while the males busied themselves with craftsmanship. There were woodling builders with tools working on trapdoors, a few zoionlings carving arrows and some plantlings making pitchers and bowls. Several species of birds chirped happily and the atmosphere was welcoming.

Raine looked up to the impressive Mount Dashar, wherein lay the Sacred Cave. It was said that the Ancient One lived on top of Mount Dashar, but that only the elders had seen his light. Raine's eyes followed the outline of the old gigantic Oak Tree that grew in front of the mountain. It was in this tree that the palace of the keepers was situated. It had a great gathering hall at the entry level and had numerous chambers, which spread throughout higher levels inside the tree trunk.

Although many keepers preferred to live in the surrounding trees, the palace served as a sanctuary for their whole race. If a threat came, all the keepers could retreat to the safety of the main dwelling.

Ah, Par. The place I once called home. The thought was strange and did not sit well with Raine anymore. Home was in the southern wilderness, the place he had grown to love more than this lovely fortress. As he floated downstream, he saw females gathered at the rocks on the riverbank washing garments. Amongst them were a few aqualings. *Females of his tribe … a rare sight.* The thought brought him back to his purpose and he grew excited. He had come to Par under the guise of finding a lifemate. It was rather ridiculous, but at least enjoyable. *It shouldn't be too difficult … all I need to do is charm some females, get the information I need and then leave.* Everyone knew Raine loved females and would be hesitant to settle with only one. *Yes, it will work…* his eyes sparkled with enthusiasm. After all, he didn't like the idea of a lifemate. It scared him witless. *Besides, if I should take one … who would make the rest of them smile?* he wondered.

He suddenly heard the laughter of an angel. It was soft and sweet. His eyes searched for the source of the music in his ears and his breath caught in his throat. There amongst the aqualings, was the most beautiful creature he had ever laid eyes on. She had light-blue hair that reached her waist and the most amazing turquoise eyes, which slanted upwards slightly. The rest of her features were small and well-sculpted. Pale grey skin was common amongst their tribe, but hers was flawless. *Spectacular,* he thought.

Raine swam with purpose towards them, a wolfish smile on his lips. He leaped out of the water with enthusiasm and then he bowed low before them in a charming way.

"Good day, lovely ladies."

They giggled and his chest swelled. With shiny, playful eyes, his gaze fell upon the lovely aqualing and he was suddenly trapped in a whirlpool. She looked at him with no particular interest, making an acknowledging gesture with her head, before quickly slipping from the rock and hurrying away. The rest of the females surrounded him and asked a million questions. They soon learned what his business was and that made them more eager to stay in his company.

Raine felt foolish. He had established the so-called reason for his visit, but now somehow regretted saying it. He was upset that the beautiful aqualing had not paid him any attention. No female had ever acted like that towards him. They always liked him, but she had dismissed him as though he was not worthy of her company. Still, he continued his pretense with the rest of the beauties surrounding him. He told them how lovely they were, complimented each one and made playful jokes, but his mind kept on wandering back to deep turquoise eyes.

Who was she? What was her name? Was she mated already? He was determined to find out.

Raine spent the rest of the afternoon walking around the city, greeting keepers and making sure everyone knew why he was there. He was welcomed amongst his tribe and shown to a guest chamber. Soon enough he was reminded to attend the feast of Solace, where many of the female aqualings would be introduced to him. As for the rest of the tribes, he did not pick up any obvious hatred, but was careful to examine the relationships between the tribes.

The afternoon passed swiftly and throughout it he hardly spent a moment alone as females fell over their feet to charm and serve him. He knew he was probably more handsome than the average male, but their eagerness made him uncomfortable.

He prepared himself for the feast and on his way there, he stopped frequently to speak to as many aqualings as possible. Soon enough he would prompt them for the answers he needed, but for now, he would just gain their trust. He knew he was part of this tribe, yet he did not feel like it. His heart directed him back to the Light Bearers.

The great hall was a short walk from his chamber and as he moved towards it, the beauty of Par in the moonlight left him spellbound. Fireflies lit up the city amongst the trees and keepers of every kind were dancing to the magical sounds of music. Some were swirling in the air, others dancing playfully on the rocks, in the trees and on the surface of the water. It was astonishing. Plantlings were swinging on flower swings and woodlings were sitting on branches playing flutes and drums. The forest came alive under their joyful celebrations and Raine found it hard to believe that this was a race on the brink of war.

As he entered the hall, his eyes scanned the area searching for her. He was intercepted by one of his tribe members, who was held in high regard. The keeper held him trapped in a meaningless conversation for a while and then directed him to one of the main tables. There he was seated next to an unexpected visitor in Par … Boforic, the dwarf, whom he met only days ago at his own outpost when he was their guest. It was an odd scene. He was seated on a custom-made chair, which was much bigger than the others and he seemed a bit squashed behind the table. Boforic winked at him as he lifted a goblet to his mouth. Some of the males engaged Raine in discussions about the outpost and then they shared some gossip. All this time, Raine's eyes kept searching the hall.

"Laddie, the bonnie lasses fall over their feet to talk to ye and I can see that ye have a charm for them, but ye doona seem much interested."

Raine stared at the dwarf with surprise. "Actually my friend, I am quite fond of their vast beauty," he replied with his wolfish smile and usual arrogant way. "They are the ones who charm me."

"Is that so, laddie? Yer eyes are nay agreeing. They're searching for someone, aye?" the dwarf asked, cocking an eyebrow.

Raine felt a bit annoyed by the dwarf's keen observation and he didn't want to acknowledge his unexpected weakness, yet denying it seemed oddly pointless. "Well, there is this one who I saw today," he reluctantly admitted.

"Ahh, she must be verra bonny then," Boforic said, clapping Raine on the shoulder and chuckling.

Not wanting to look as foolish as he felt, Raine shrugged his shoulders and replied, "I suppose so."

Boforic's whole upper body shook as he laughed. "Och, nay laddie! Tis nay a bad thing to find a lifemate. Ye don't have to be scared. Aye, tis a beautiful gift nature gives ye."

Boforic just called him scared. Scared … of a female … of all things. Was the dwarf daft? He wasn't even scared of Maple and many males should be. Besides, all females loved him. He didn't say anything out of respect for their guest, but he really wanted to throttle the dwarf.

A few more females sought Raine out and he tried to pay attention to them, but grew irritated by all their antics. Then he saw her, in a dark corner, almost hidden. Just as he was about to excuse himself, Boforic's eyes followed his own. "Och, aye laddie, she is verra bonny. Now I see how a charmer such as ye fell down the rabbit hole."

Raine frowned in irritation at the dwarf. Guest or not, the dwarf was out of line and Raine had used up all his politeness with him.

"Say Boforic, were you not supposed to be with the Fey now? That was where you were heading the last time I saw you."

"Aye laddie, I did say that, didn't I? But after I forgot me precious axe in Par, I had to return. Canna leave it behind, ye see."

Raine opened his mouth to say something, but the dwarf winked at him again and dismissed him with a wave of his hand. Raine pushed out his chest, got up and headed straight towards her. He found himself staring at the loveliness before him, not quite believing that she was real. She enchanted him.

"Hi, I am Raine, son of Cloud. What's your name?"

She looked up at him shyly. "Hi, I am Dew, daughter of Mist."

"Would you care to dance with me, Dew?"

Dew looked up at him through long black lashes and said softly, "No, thank you."

Raine almost choked. He had never been turned down before. "Why not?" he wanted to know.

"I know who you are and I'm not interested in your careless flirtations." For a small shy-looking thing, she sure had courage, he thought. She was not a bit intimidated by him, nor moved by his presence. *Very odd* … the first female that did not fall for his charm. Instead of feeling hurt, Raine was proud of her.

"Ok, then," he smiled. "I will just sit here and talk with you, without flirting of course."

"Why?" she asked.

"Well, because you captivate me," he said without hesitation.

Dew was puzzled. "Perhaps I don't want you to. I don't like attention and prefer to keep to myself."

Raine was beginning to enjoy the challenge. "I think you are worthy of my attention."

Dew pushed out her chin and looked him straight in the eyes. "I don't think I'm not worthy of attention, I just don't want any."

He frowned, confused by her answer. Seeing his confusion, she sighed. "If you pay attention to me, it means the whole village will notice and I don't like that idea one bit. I've heard about your so-called quest and I wish you good hunting, but please exclude me. My duties here are far more important than being the possible lifemate of an arrogant male."

Raine's scowl deepened. For a moment, he was speechless. "What duties would that be?" he asked, when he finally found his voice.

Her turquoise eyes sparkled with irritation. "I'm a nursemaid. I take care of orphans. So you see, as an orphan myself, I am not moved by males who think they are more important than anyone else, when the younglings actually are."

Raine's heart skipped a beat. She was an orphan just like he was. She could see right through his pretense. All these years he had used his good looks and charm to hide his own loneliness. His cobalt blue eyes sparkled seriousness that he only revealed in battle. "So you lost your parents too? I lost mine before the outposts were created, in the days when many foreign species crossed into Equilibria. They were killed while tending an area close to the border. It was their death and those of many others at the time, that convinced the elders to create the teams and the outposts," he confessed to her.

Dew was stunned. She certainly had not expected this boastful male to be sincere or serious. He was an orphan just like her and his parents died in the same way her parents had. Now his behavior made sense. As hard as she tried to hide, he was determined to stand out; both of them were trying to find a way to fit in.

"I don't remember you from the orphan chambers," she said softly, without a trace of her previous annoyance.

"That's because I wasn't raised there. I was chosen as a youngling to become a warrior. I was raised separately and later I joined the rest of my outpost team," he told her.

Raine knew at that moment that he would never be the same again. He had met his match. She was his complete opposite, yet they were the same in so many ways. Perhaps that was why he was so drawn to her. *Tis nay a bad thing to find a lifemate ...* The words of the dwarf echoed in his mind as the thought took hold. Strangely it did not choke him anymore. Not like it used to. Instead, he had never felt surer about anything. He knew when he looked into her eyes again, that she had realised it too. His eyes dropped to her mouth and without a thought he bent down and kissed her. Deep down, a part of him objected, but he just couldn't help himself.

Suddenly roars of voices and claps went up from the crowd. Amongst them, was the very loud praise of Boforic. Raine realised his mistake. *Oh no!* He just claimed his lifemate. Right there, in front of everyone and he had not even shown Dew the necessary respect by asking her to be his lifemate. The kiss however sealed their fate, as was the way of the keepers. There was no going back now.

Raine went into a state of panic, his chest suddenly tight, and anxious thoughts rushed through his mind. He had not anticipated this. He had risked his quest. How would he be able to get the information he was sent to find? He would not be able to flirt with the females anymore. Could he trust Dew with his deadly secret? He would have to take her back to the outpost with him. It was expected of him to do so. Before their departure, there would be the exchange of binding vows, similar to the one he made to the Light Bearers, just days ago. *You fool, Raine!* This time it was not his charming nature that got him into trouble, but his serious side that he had kept hidden for so long.

As his eyes found those deep turquoise pools again, he found himself calming down. Dew looked up at him with big tears. He knew she was just as confused as he was. Perhaps she was shamed and angry with him.

"I'm sorry," he whispered to her. "I didn't mean for this to happen. But it feels right with you."

She didn't say a word, but turned around on her heel and fled from the hall, her reaction a plain rejection of his claim.

He heard the loud gasps behind him, as he automatically chased after her. *How could she reject me in front of everyone? But then again, I claimed her in front of everyone without her consent.* His emotions were in chaos and his thoughts totally scrambled. He knew that leaving Par and the younglings she cared for would be painful for her, but he had no intention of leaving her behind. He knew without a doubt that she belonged with him and he suddenly did not feel sorry for his very public display, although he was worried about the consequences of it. Would she accept their fate, or would she leave him known as the fool amongst their kind? How was he going to explain this to Aire? His commander would be furious. And would his mate be able to forgive him for robbing her of the life she was used to? He hurried along the footpath, which she was briskly walking on. "Dew! Wait, please wait," he shouted, but she just kept increasing her pace.

Then she entered a chamber and slammed the wooden trapdoor shut. When he reached it, he first hesitated and then knocked. Silence. "Dew, please open the door. I know you're in there. Please let's talk."

"Go away," she countered.

"Dew, you know that's not possible. You are my mate now. There's no going back," he added the last part almost in a whisper.

"I don't want to be your mate," she replied willfully.

Raine sighed as he pulled his hand through his spiky hair. How ironic. He could pick almost any female, yet the one he chose did not want him. "Dew, I'm sorry. I didn't expect or ask for this. You know that the pull between mates is strong. I felt it and so did you."

She opened the door and his breath was once again stolen by the vision of her. She peered up at him through wet eyelashes and he felt angry for being responsible for her pain. "Raine, son of Cloud, you are the most arrogant, selfish, overbearing male that I've ever met."

She practically spat out the words at him as she pointed and pressed her finger to his chest.

"Ouch! That hurt," he said with a grin. "But I deserve it."

"Don't try your charms on me. I'm not done yet," she informed him. He frowned. Was his lifemate a Maple type? That was not a welcoming thought.

"Did you even once consider the implications, before you claimed me in front of everyone? You didn't even have the honour of asking me if I wanted this."

Raine winced at her scolding. It was hurtful, but he knew it was true. He had not thought at all, he had only acted. She continued her onslaught. "The younglings need me." Her voice broke as she uttered the last words. That was more than he could stand. Raine pulled her to his chest and she sobbed into it, while she beat her two tiny fists against him.

He held her tight and whispered next to her ear, "I need you too. More than you could ever imagine." He stroked her hair and allowed her to release all her pain and anger upon him. Raine vowed at that moment, that he would never cause her pain again.

Dew felt so angry and confused. How could he just walk into her life and turn it upside down. He didn't even give her a choice. Yet, she knew that his pained declaration was true. He did need her, she sensed it. She wondered if he was as frightened as she was. As much as she wanted to run away, she knew there would be no escaping. There was no denying the pull between lifemates. She was thankful they had similar backgrounds. Still, Dew couldn't rid herself of the annoying thought that he was a charmer. If Raine continued in his old ways, he would make an absolute fool of her.

His voice penetrated the thickness in her head, which was caused by her tears. "If it is any consolation, I was humiliated when you rejected me in front of everyone," he said.

Her turquoise pools trapped him again. "You deserved it," she whispered.

"Yes, I did," he admitted softly. "Please forgive me, Dew. I promise I'll make it up to you." He took her lovely face in his hands and looked deeply into her eyes. "For so many years, I was confused and lost, always trying to prove myself. Looking at you, I know I've finally found peace. Will you please be my lifemate?"

Raine was trembling. This was the worst possible time to find a lifemate, but his whole elemental being knew that there was no way that he could give up his other half. He held his breath as he waited for her answer.

Dew lifted her hand to his and their fingertips touched, their elemental nature reacted and their fingertips melted together like two water droplets forming a single one. It was undeniable. He was her mate.

"Nature has cast its lot. To reject it would be foolish. Yes Raine, I will be your mate," she said softly.

Raine uttered a sigh of relief and kissed the top of her head. "Thank you. I vow to never cause you pain again." He almost didn't recognise his own voice as emotion filled him. "I will inform the elders of our decision. Tomorrow we will take our vows," he added quickly. He wasn't taking any chances, just in case his mate decided to flee again.

Later, as Raine stepped into his own chamber, his heart soared within him.

He did not get another opportunity to talk to Dew the following day. Raine left his chambers early to inform the tribe elders of their decision, and Dew was swept up by the older females to prepare her for their binding ceremony.

Chapter 11

Nightfall came swiftly and Raine walked up and down, waiting for Dew's arrival. Tonight they would come together under the moon of Solace to take their binding vows. He felt nervous and the crowd that gathered under the old Oak Tree did not make it any easier. Due to all the havoc he had caused the previous evening, their binding ceremony held the interest of almost every keeper in Par. Gossip travelled quickly. He looked over the members of his tribe, who stood in equal anticipation. At the back, he spotted the dwarf and gave him an acknowledging nod. It seemed as though Boforic was acutely aware of everything happening around him. Raine smiled as he realised that Boforic also didn't seem to miss a celebration.

He looked up as a twig snapped and there she stood, looking like an enchanting water nymph. Dew's beauty was unmatched and Raine thought he was dreaming. Pearls were draped in an elegant crown around her head and she wore an equally stunning silver and turquoise gown. Her eyes met his and then he was lost in the whirlpool again. When she stepped up next to him, they faced each other and he took her hands in his. He heard Tsunami announce the binding and then the elder's voice grew vague. He was only aware of her. A hand touched his shoulder and then the eyes of the elder bored into him. "Speak your vow, Raine, son of Cloud," he heard him say. Raine cleared his throat and hoped that his voice would come out steady.

"Dew, daughter of Mist. To you, oh fair one; I pledge my heart, my protection and my life. I, Raine, son of Cloud, choose to serve

you in love and be your lifemate in all instances, until nature claims us back to our elemental forms. From this moment forth I am one with you as you are one with me, bound by the element of water, for all time."

Dew repeated her vow to him and then a great feast was held in their name.

Every keeper congratulated them. The older ones seemed especially overjoyed with the new pairing. Dew had to endure a few terrible glances from the other females, but she paid little attention to them. Just when she thought it was all over, almost every male wanted to dance with her. Across the hall, Raine's eyes followed her. He often smiled at her, but she could see that he too was very nervous.

Later that evening they returned to Dew's chamber. Raine felt the nervous pull growing in his belly. He knew that he had to discuss his current circumstances with her, but he did not know where to start. He was worried that she would not understand. He also did not know to what extent he could trust her. What if she did not understand and betrayed him to the council?

He admired her as she moved around the chamber, seemingly aimlessly and without any specific purpose. He wondered how she felt. After a few casual glances and polite gestures, Raine decided to settle the uneasiness between them.

As she glided past him again, he reached out and grabbed her hand. He tilted her chin upwards and looked into her eyes. "Dew, are you still angry with me? I'm really sorry that I turned your life upside down, but I'm not sorry about my choice in you. You are my lifemate. I'm certain of this. I know it is expected of you to return with me to the outpost, but since I've failed so miserably to begin with, I will now show you the proper respect. Please will you come back with me to the outpost," he asked, in his gentlest voice.

She stared at him for a while, before she spoke. "I know we are meant to be together and yes, I will return with you, but only on one condition." Raine's heart missed a beat. This did not sound good. She was about to give him an ultimatum. "Promise me that you will stop flirting with other females. I do not want to be shamed by your carelessness."

A crooked smile formed around his mouth as he relaxed. "Of course. I am a joined male now. Besides, you've spoiled me for all other females. I only think of your loveliness now."

Her eyes twinkled as she smiled back at him. "Good. Then it's settled."

Raine stroked his chin in deep thought. After considering his options, he decided to come clean and share everything with his mate. He told her about the Light Bearers and their plans to restore peace, and also of him messing up his quest by falling in love with her. Dew laughed at first and accepted everything without hesitation. She did not push him for any more information and he was humbled by her faith in him and his choices.

Then she casually announced, "Perhaps I can help you with your quest." She turned around, fumbled in a hole in the wall of the wooden chamber and pulled out a scroll. She handed it to him with a smile. It was a map of the secret entrances to the underground tunnels, which connected all the dwellings in Par. Raine studied it and shook his head in disbelief. He gave her a hard look.

"Where did you get this? Are you involved with the rebellion?"

Dew rolled her eyes. "You think I am a spy? The answer is no. I just saw some aqualings snooping around suspiciously the other night. So I followed them down to the creek where I overheard them discussing an invasion of the city. They seem to think that aqualings have an advantage when it comes to the invasion of Par. From what I overheard, they have already made the northern outpost their stronghold. I am not sure what happened to the keepers there. They had gotten this map from a zoionling. Do you think this means that the zoionlings are also considering an invasion of Par?"

"I'm not sure. It sounds likely. We need to get back to our Aire as soon as possible with this information." Raine was feeling apprehensive. "But how did you get a hold of the map?"

She smiled shyly. "After they had their discussion, I saw them hide the map under a marked rock for their contact to find. When they left, I stole it before it fell into the wrong hands."

Raine's eyes were filled with admiration for her. "You are very brave and I am truly honoured to be your mate. It was a dangerous thing you did and not the kind you should consider again," he remarked, rebuking her with a smile. She didn't seem the least bit bothered by his concern. Instead, she peeked back at him with a devilish gleam in her eyes.

Raine found great pleasure in her attempt to show stubbornness and tried his best not to laugh. "I still don't understand the origins of the map," he said.

Dew gave a shrug. "It must have been stolen from the Sacred Cave where all the sacred scrolls are kept."

Raine's smile was way too big for his face. "I think you are right."

Dew frowned. "What will we do with the map?"

"We will take it to Aire. He will know best. Besides, if we do succeed in returning it to the Sacred Cave, someone else might steal it again. As you said, we cannot risk it falling into the wrong hands at a time like this," he replied.

The following morning, they said their goodbyes to everyone and Dew spent a few last moments with the younglings. Just before they left, she requested a quick stop at the dwelling of her friend Fern – a plantling. Raine couldn't help but notice that Fern was slender and tall for her kind. Her big green eyes shone like emeralds and were wide set in her heart shaped face. This complimented her green hair, which was streaked with golden highlights. Her gown looked classy, made of evergreen leaves, while a gold twig crown rested on her head. Because Fern was so young, he found it strange when she gave Dew a bag full of herbs and medicines. Normally healers were older than Fern and they certainly were not as well decorated as she was.

Once they had returned on the footpath, Raine asked, "Why is your healer friend so young and well adorned? I find that rather strange."

Dew moved gracefully in her purple gown and smiled. "She's the cousin of Ivy the Gentle, elder of the plantlings. She showed interest in the healing arts as a youngling and Ivy permitted her training. Obviously, as she is under Ivy's care, she needs to dress well."

Raine bowed jokingly before Dew and said, "You are not only wise, but well-connected too. I am beginning to think that I do not deserve such a wonderful mate. With a possible battle at hand, her medicines and friendship could mean a great deal to the Light Bearers."

Dew punched him playfully as they jumped into the stream that would lead them to the southern outpost.

After a few hours of travelling, they met up with the rest of the team at the main dwelling of the outpost. When Raine entered the chamber with his hand in Dew's, everybody stared at them in disbelief. Even Aire was temporarily speechless. Nobody had expected Raine to return with a female.

After a long silence, Aire cocked his head sideways, and finally broke the stillness in his direct, no-nonsense approach. "Welcome back Raine. I trust all went well. Who is the lovely female accompanying you and what is her purpose here?"

Raine gave them a huge smile, looking like the happiest male in Equilibria. He stepped forward and bowed low before his brethren.

"It is good to be home. Meet my lifemate, Dew. She will be joining us."

After he uttered the word *lifemate*, Maple's breath caught in her throat and Muddy turned a strange brown colour. Lilly swayed, blacked out and nearly reached the floor, but Shadow caught her just in time. The animal protector was the only one who seemed unaffected.

Sparks flew off Aire and his eyes turned dark. Raine quickly moved in front of Dew and held up a hand as if to stop Aire from striking them with lightning. "Wow! Stop! Relax, okay. Let me explain. It's not as bad as you think."

Holding Dew's hand tight in his, Raine explained what happened in Par. He told them everything and then he handed over the map to Aire, who calmed down notably. The commander stared into the distance, leaving everyone to wonder what he was thinking.

After moments of silence, Aire spoke again. "I never thought I would say it, but congratulations Raine and Dew. And well done on your quest. You both did well. We welcome and accept you in our family, Dew. It is an honour to meet the one who has stolen our brother's heart."

Aire moved forward and dragged Dew out from behind Raine's back, where all could see her and then he gave her a welcoming hug. Everyone was surprised when Maple jumped up next and hugged Dew, also welcoming her. Lilly clutched her hands in her own and then whispered a soft hello.

Muddy gave her an awkward hug and slapped Raine playfully on the shoulder. "Cover me with jewels and rub my skin with moss," he said, shaking his head in astonishment.

"Now all those shiny clothes of yours will finally serve a purpose," he added with mischief in his eyes.

Raine cocked an eyebrow at him and asked dryly, "And what would that be?"

"Why, but to reflect the lovely image named Dew, of course. You didn't think I was talking about you, did you? I should have figured that nature would mate you with someone prettier than yourself." His smile engulfed his face and everyone shared a chuckle. Shadow was the only one who bowed low before her without saying a word.

That night they had a small feast to celebrate the safe return of the spies. Shadow and Maple gave everyone an update on their quests, while the rest of the team listened attentively. Later the feast turned into a celebration of everyone's successes and the pairing of Raine and Dew. Aire's face gave away his emotions, revealing to all how proud he was of his team. He never doubted them, but he never bargained on a new team member either. There was laughter, happiness, and everyone shared in the joy of their new sister.

Aire looked at them and realised that his worries were actualising faster than what he was comfortable with. If rebel groups had already invaded the other outposts, only the southern outpost remained unaffected. Would the remaining rebel groups try to invade their outpost to make it their stronghold? Perhaps, although all knew that theirs was furthest away from Par and the area was the most difficult to survive in, compared to the other outposts. The worst of it all was the fact that the forest was dying. He couldn't bear to think what would happen if they failed to stop the war and return peace. *Were evil increases, death comes swiftly.*

Aire was thankful when the laughter of his teammates snapped him out of his gloomy thoughts. Their victory was small, but well-deserved and for tonight he would relax with his team and be happy. Soon he would share his insight and prepare them for what might come next. Aire smiled and held up a goblet while he made a tribute. Everyone joined with their own goblets and then they all shouted together, "For light and honour!"

Chapter 12

oforic stretched lazily and opened his eyes slowly. Through barely opened lids, he could see that the light was dim in the cave. Six pairs of bright coloured stones were staring at him. *Bright eyes,* he thought. He jumped up in surprise, gave a startled cry and pulled his axe out from behind him. He lifted it up above his head and let out a fierce battle cry. He blinked for a moment and then the fog cleared from his head as he realised that it was only the three lads who were hovering over him in curiosity.

The young males jumped back, frightened. Boforic expected them to laugh at his reaction, but saw that he had scared them instead. "Sorry lads, I thought ye were some kind of strange wild animal."

Slowly smiles appeared.

"We didn't mean to startle you," said Airon.

Dusty sighed in relief and slowly started breathing again. "Thank goodness," he said. "For a moment there I thought we were going to be dwarf food."

Boforic frowned and giggled. "Dwarf food, aye laddie? Ye hardly have meat on ye bones."

Everybody laughed and the mood turned lighter.

Boforic strapped his belt and positioned his axe in place. "A new day has dawned. Tis the last sunrise before the council this night, we must get moving if we don't wanna miss it."

Dusty looked at him with big eyes and said, "But we didn't break our fast yet."

The dwarf stroked his beard. "Aye lad, I ken ye right. Me tummy is rumbly too. Let's make haste about it and get moving."

He pulled his bag closer, dug into it and pulled out three red apples. Using a dagger, he cut them into small pieces and shared them out. Drizzle supplied them with fresh water and then they were ready for the next part of their journey.

As they exited the cave, the sun was rising like a big fireball over the horizon. It gave bright yellow waves of light. Airon had his normal big grin and Drizzle also shared a crooked smile, while pointing his finger at Dusty. Boforic's gaze rested on the earthling and he too smirked, because Dusty shone brightly as the rays of the sun lit up the glittered sand particles in his skin. He looked glorious.

"Ye look bonny lad," Boforic joked.

Dusty lifted an eyebrow. "I think not! No male should be called beautiful." Now everyone chuckled and with that, the journey to the Sacred Cave resumed.

Not even five minutes into their walk, curious Airon tugged on the dwarf's pants. "Thank you for sharing the ancient legend with us. I couldn't close my eyes last night. All the time I thought about the Light Bearers and their bravery."

The other two keepers quickly agreed and soon they were discussing the incidents of the three spies. They talked with admiration and ever so often, one would try to mimic an action that took place.

Dusty popped a few wild berries that he had plucked from a nearby bush into his mouth. "You know, now I understand why Raven is such a dare devil. She takes after Shadow. I think all the young males are scared of her," he mumbled as he shook his head.

"Do you think they will make us Light Bearers too?" the earthling asked excitedly. His question got the attention of Drizzle and Airon, all of them considering the possibility.

Boforic glanced at them briefly and then cut them off with a flat reply, "Mayhap. We will see."

The males were overjoyed with the events so far and Boforic knew that they were excited to hear the next part of the tale. Still he kept them waiting a bit longer.

Finally shy Drizzle spoke. "Will you please tell us more?"

Boforic smiled and wondered how the lads had gotten under his skin so quickly. He hadn't felt so alive in years. Spending time with them made him feel important again. "Aye lad, we have a few more hours. I will tell ye more."

The three keepers danced in joy and skipped with excitement over the grassy fields that were filled with flowering bushes. Fresh dew glittered on the small purple flowers of the heather bushes and their lovely scent filled the morning air. While they happily enjoyed the scenery, Boforic took them back in time again.

Another morning had passed since the Light Bearers had been reunited. Aire had informed his team of the possible dangers that they might face and everyone was on edge, not knowing what to expect. At midday, they all gathered at the creek to hold council and discuss their options.

Aire walked up and down and finally spun around rapidly, forming a small whirlwind. Maple found herself in the middle of the dust cloud. She coughed a few times and rubbed her nose frantically to get rid of the tickle the dust caused her senses. Aire, seemingly unaware of the discomfort he caused her, looked up and frowned at her reaction. Then he removed the map from his pocket and spread it open on the ground for all to see.

He hunkered in front of it and pointed to the secret tunnels that lead into the main hall of Par. "I'm sure that the rebels were planning to use these secret tunnels to gain entrance to the city. I never knew of their existence and I suspect very few others do. It's a good thing that Dew stopped the plans of the aqualing rebels. Without the map, it will be impossible to guess where these entrances are. We'll keep this information secret and hidden. I don't want this map to fall into the wrong hands again. Some rebels might still try to take our outpost to use it as their base. I wish it was avoidable, but after what you've discovered at the other outposts and in the city, I am beginning to believe that a battle might be inevitable. Shadow, it is time for you and Argon to do some scouting over our lands."

Shadow and Argon left, while the rest of the team remained at the creek. After a few hours, the Light Bearers became aware of Argon's presence, as he circled in the air and gave his familiar cry to announce their return. Once he landed, Shadow slipped easily from Argon and walked casually toward the others. His demeanor was relaxed as always but his raven eyes held a daunting colour of darkness in the midday sun. Something was wrong.

Shadow stood before his fellow brethren but kept his gaze on the ground. Aire shifted uncomfortably on his stone seat. "What news do you bring, Shadow?"

The warrior lifted his head slowly, his eyes scanned over all his friends, and then he rested his gaze on their commander. He responded in a flat tone. "Rebel forces are approaching from the east."

Aire looked at him intensely. "Who?"

Shadow cleared his throat. "Plantlings. A dozen of them. I recognised one of them from the training camp in Par. I believe we called him Bushy the Edgy."

Lilly grasped her hands together and quickly covered her mouth with both of them. "No! You just frightened the curl right out of my hair. His reputation precedes him."

Maple frowned upon Lilly's remark; obviously Lilly would think anyone dangerous. She inwardly shook her head at the plantling's fragileness, but said nothing.

Shadow remained expressionless, but his eyes grew darker by the moment. Aire nodded quietly and then asked, "How much time do we have?"

The zoionling removed an arrow from his quiver and inspected it carefully. Then he pulled out a dagger from his belt to carve an inscription on the arrow.

"They should be here by nightfall."

"Good, that gives us a few hours," said Raine.

Lilly tapped her fingers together in a nervous manner. "Bushy is unpredictable. Even as a youngling he often disregarded the instructions of the older keepers. I think rebellion was always part of his nature and now he has free reign. I am afraid that his natural rebellious streak, mixed with the taste of power, could make him an unkind opponent."

Raine grumbled. "They would be foolish to attack us."

Shadow approved as he chuckled softly. "Foolish, indeed."

Aire frowned at them both. "Are you so eager to fight?"

Shadow settled lazily against a tree. He looked at Aire and shook his head. "Not eager, just ready." Raine agreed with him, showing off a pair of dimples.

They used the rest of the afternoon to discuss possible battle tactics. Dew and Lilly prepared food for everyone, but Maple decided to join the males in their planning. Females of their kind were not normally interested in fighting, but the males were outnumbered as it was. Maple reasoned that an extra pair of hands could do no harm, although she was a bit frightened. A vision of a one-eared Maple popped up in her head. The idea of becoming battle scarred was repulsive, but she was going to fight and no one could stop her. After all, none of the males who had been scarred in some or other way had difficulty in preserving their self-worth. She briefly considered that they might reject her. She was prepared to defend her decision, if one of the males objected. Strangely, none of them paid her any attention.

She heard Aire say that the rebels would probably invade the dwelling from all directions, to trap them. Many strategies were weighed, but in the end, they decided to remain hidden and capture their enemies in booby traps. Should the rebels become aware of the traps, they would attack the moment they had reached the centre of the dwelling. In doing so, they would have the element of surprise.

Maple got excited and spoke before she realised what she was doing. "We will probably need some cages, like the ones the woodling rebels in the east used. If we only keep them captured in chambers, they might escape like I did." Suddenly all gazes zoomed in on her and more than one male frowned. In fact, all but Shadow did; he was the only one who knew her true strength, she decided.

She paled, but had no intention of backing off. Instead, she lifted her chin in defiance. Shadow gave her a quirky smile and nodded his head slowly. "That's a great idea Maple. Would you be able to forge wooden cages if I tell you how they should look?"

Maple's smile almost swallowed up her whole face as she thankfully stared back at Shadow. "Yes! Of course, I can. I am a woodling. All I need to do is ask and the trees will gladly assist."

Aire grunted. "Well, that settles it. Maple, you are responsible for the cages. Muddy, you are responsible for holes in the ground. Make them deep enough so that our captives will not be able to escape from them."

He looked around and signaled Lilly closer. "Lilly, I need you to cover the holes in the ground with leaves. Also, call upon the plants to weave fine nets from stem fibres. You and Muddy must work together to cover the nets and hide them from the eyes of our enemies. The idea is to capture them the moment they step onto them."

"So you are going to let us fight them?" asked Maple, her eyes sparkling.

Aire smiled at her. "Yes Maple, this battle belongs to the Light Bearers. As I told you before, we are warriors and that certainly includes the females too. Unless you are afraid that you might lose your enchanting beauty, then we will exempt you from it."

Maple could not help herself and threw her arms around Aire. He looked surprised but whirled her around into a dust cloud. She sneezed uncontrollably and everyone laughed.

When Dew approached them with the food, everyone grabbed something to eat, while they remained in deep conversation. Next Aire instructed Shadow to attack from the air and then he concluded, "Raine, Dew and I will give them a storm. Wind and water combined is a destructive force. That should destroy their defences and once we've captured them, we'll interrogate them."

Chapter 13

ightfall came swiftly and the stronghold of the southern outpost lay desolated and created the impression that no one occupied it. Shadow's dark eyes scanned the area from his vantage point high in the trees. The air was thick with anticipation. It was quiet, almost too quiet. Then he caught a movement out the corner of his eye. A branch swayed and he saw them approaching slowly from all directions. The Light Bearers' assumption had been correct – the enemy's intention was to encircle and trap them.

Shadow gave the signal of a nightingale. On the ground his brethren were hiding amongst the dirt and leaves. He searched for Aire's presence not far from his own hideout and then he heard his commander reply with the hoot of an owl. Concentrating, he pulled out an arrow from his quiver and aimed. Slowly he released it and it swooshed through the air with stealth and grace. After a brief thud, a big plantling fell down to his knees and then tipped over in a silent fall. *One down, eleven to go*, he said softly.

After Shadow's signal, Aire peered through the trees. Using hand signals, he alerted the rest of his team to move towards the centre of the dwelling. His mouth fell into a hard line as he crawled through the leaves. *They won't know what hit them*, he thought.

Maple was crouching low when she heard the signal and knew it was time. A cold chill ran down her spine. She clung to the blade Shadow had given her and, although fearful, she was determined to take out at least one enemy. Barely finishing the thought, she looked up and stared straight into the eyes of resentment. Her pulse quickened and her blood ran cold. Although her enemy was physically attractive as all the keepers, his huge build made him look very frightening. His mouth curved into a menacing smile as he swung a big wooden hammer towards her.

Maple's senses flared and she moved with unexpected speed. She rolled over, jumped back onto her feet and then raised her arm to swing her blade in an upward thrust. She struck the plantling with a blow on the head, knocking him out cold. *That was unexpected ... you were supposed to slice him open Maple, not knock him out*, she told herself.

The stealth master smiled as he watched Maple defeat her foe. He pulled out another arrow, but then all hell broke loose as one of the foes stepped into a trap. Getting caught in the net and being jerked up high into the air, he cried out, "Trap," and alerted his fellow warriors. Angry plantlings stormed into the dwelling, looking around in puzzlement. When Aire, Raine and Muddy leaped out of the darkness onto them, covered in grime and looking wild, they realised that they were under attack.

The Light Bearers cried, "For light and honour" and then the crash of steel on steel echoed through the night. Arrows whizzed through the air as Shadow dispatched them at a rapid pace, taking out another three of the rogues. *Six down ... six to go.*

Shadow's eyes sought out his brothers. From his hideout, he could assist them easily with his arrows. He watched Muddy wielding his blade with skillfulness and certainty. Earthlings were one with the natural metals and everything that was forged from them. His rival gave him a few scratches with his blade, but Muddy had the upper hand. He was light-footed, giving blow after blow. Then he swung his blade down and sliced across the stomach of his opponent. The plantling stumbled back and fell to the ground.

Lilly looked around anxiously. She knew she was the weakest keeper of their team and at that moment, she wished she had more courage and strength. She heard Raine shout out, "Lilly, behind you!" Then terror froze her to the spot. Looking over her small shoulder, a fierce plantling with green hair and shiny amber eyes grabbed her arm. Lilly did the only thing she could and clawed into his pale green flesh. He cried out and backhanded her across the face in defence.

Clumsily she reached between the folds in her dress and pulled out a small dagger. She clenched the hilt of it in her hand and remembered Shadow's words, "Don't hesitate and strike hard." Without further thought, she did exactly that and stabbed the rogue in his belly. She caught him off-guard and he was unable to block her accurate strike. His hands darted to the wound and he fell down at her feet. Lilly stared in horror at the work of her hands and tears sprung to her eyes. She covered her mouth with both her hands and tried not to puke all over the place. The remains of the plantling immediately dried out like a withered plant. Lilly watched as the once beautiful perfect body quickly lost its form and turned into nothing more than a broken stalk. She looked up and saw how bravely her friends were fighting. She convinced herself that if they could do it, she could too. She got ready to defend herself again.

Dew watched Raine fight a big villain. His cobalt eyes shone bright in the darkness. Her mate moved like a leopard, with skill and elegance. He delivered some heavy blows to the ribs of his attacker. Raine's reflective clothes proved to be an advantage to him, because they confused his attacker. The rogue might as well have been practicing against a mirror, because every time he plunged forward, he frowned, not knowing if he was pointing his weapon at Raine or himself. After some time, he got used to his opponent's rare distraction. It was then that the rogue reached over his shoulder and a blade flashed in the moonlight. Fear rose in Dew's throat and she held her breath. Raine lost his balance for a moment as his opponent hit him hard with the backside of the blade on his shoulder, but the aqualing was not defeated. He moved quickly and defeated the warrior. He captured the foe's hands behind his back and fastened them with a braided grass thread, flashing Dew a swift reassuring smile.

Her eyes followed an arrow that whooshed passed her and then a pale green hand grabbed her around her middle. She screamed. Raine's eyes found hers and they held for a moment, then he moved to defend her. He charged with his blade lifted high above his head and the sound of crashing waves filled the air. Her attacker laughed in her ear and she nearly choked with fear.

"You want to save your female, huh?" he challenged with a deep voice. He tossed her to the ground as his blade met Raine's. The rogue's sword moved swiftly and Raine saw it too late. He knocked Raine's weapon out of his hand and it fell. He blocked the next blow with his forearm and the blade sank into his skin. Dew heard him shout, "Arrggh!"

Dew screamed again and ran forward. She grabbed the blade Raine had dropped and, without realising the dangerous position she had placed herself in, she charged the rogue and stabbed him. He didn't see it coming and fell to the ground. Her heart was pounding in her chest as she knelt in the dirt next to her mate. She tore off a piece of her dress and wrapped it around his wound.

"It's okay. I'll take care of you," she said lovingly to him.

Aire stood his ground as the rebel commander, Bushy the Edgy, charged at him with a huge battle-axe. *He must have gotten the design from the dwarves, only they are renowned for such monstrous weapons*, Aire told himself. He smiled boldly at the rogue as they moved in a circle, sizing each other up. Watching … waiting to see who would make the first move.

Bushy's green eyes sparked with menace. "Give up your dwelling, airling. Defending it is a lost cause. Either you give it to me or you will soon be in a battle with the earthlings or your own kind."

Aire kept his gaze steady on Bushy. "What's the matter Bushy, afraid I will scar your handsome face? I'll take my chances. Your greed will not destroy our lives," he replied.

Bushy charged forward and swung the heavy axe towards him.

Aire moved fast and dodged it with ease, then he twisted rapidly round and round. The whirlwind he created was filled with dust and Bushy had difficulty seeing. Aire spun upward in the dust cloud and jumped down on Bushy, causing him to fall flat on his back and drop his weapon. Aire leaped onto Bushy, landing with his knees into his chest, and delivered a couple of blows to his face and a couple more to his ribs, leaving his enemy powerless and defeated. "Sorry about your looks, but I tried to warn you," Aire said, almost sounding regretful.

The plantling, whom Maple knocked out, got up and the two last who remained standing charged, trying to defend their commander. Aire jumped to his feet and shouted, "Storm," eyeing Raine and Dew. The two aqualings joined him and they grabbed each other's hands, forming a small circle. The markings on their wrists glowed in the darkness as they spun around and up.

Suddenly wind and rain came down crashing and lightning shot through the dark sky. With the sound of crashing waves and thunder, the dwelling became a creepy place. The three plantlings looked around in terror and darted in all directions. Two fell into one of Muddy's holes and Shadow took down the last one, shooting an arrow into his leg. One by one, they had cut down the rebels. Injured warriors lay strewn across the ground. It was done. The Light Bearers had fought bravely and succeeded in defending their outpost.

They rounded up their enemies and locked them in the cages. Dew fetched the medicine bag and took care of everyone's wounds. She spent some extra time with Raine, because she had to stitch up his gash. Keepers healed quickly when nurtured with the elements that they were related to. With a few extra cups of water, Raine's arm would heal faster and if Muddy rubbed a few grains of sand on his scratches, they would too. When she finally finished with the Light Bearers, Lilly helped her to give some herbs and liquid remedies to their prisoners.

Aire let out a sigh of relief as he looked at his team. "You fought bravely Light Bearers. I'm proud of you. Unfortunately, not all survived and blood was spilled this night."

Lilly let out a sob and his eyes found hers. "You did well tonight, Lilly."

She lowered her head slowly and spoke softly. "I know, but he was my own kind and I killed him."

Aire nodded with understanding. "Do not condemn yourself. It was either you or him, and he did not hesitate to strike."

Lilly stared back at him with conviction. She realised what he said was true.

Their commander then looked at them all. "I know your hearts are as heavy as mine. None of us ever expected to battle against other keepers. Keepers were made to care for the forest. We're supposed to live and work together in harmony. Even tonight, we've proven our dependency upon each other. The Light Bearers conquered because we fought as one, and the plantlings were defeated because they did not have the diverse strengths that we have. Together keepers are strong, but divided we fall. We're not supposed to be our own enemies. It's not natural. This time calls for us to do what we despise. What else can we do but defend our existence? We have to press forward for the sake of Equilibria, for the survival of our kind."

Everyone listened to him as his voice travelled in the stillness of the night. Even the prisoners, that hung in their elevated cages in the tree, listened. An uncomfortable silence stretched through the still night air, as each one pondered his words.

Chapter 14

The following morning, the Light Bearers gathered at the base of the tree from which the cages hung. It was time to get answers. They lowered them to the ground. The plantlings still looked beaten up, but something was different about them. Their previous menacing expressions had faded and they appeared friendlier. Aire looked at his prisoners and wondered what brought on their change of attitude. Perhaps it was a trick. He frowned and spoke to the commander.

"Bushy, I trust that you find your accommodation comfortable. I hope that we can talk like civilised keepers and not like enemies."

Bushy nodded slowly. "Yes, you're right. We behaved uncivilised. We're sorry. Forgive us for attacking your peaceful post. We didn't realise that there were keepers who still believed in the old ways."

Aire stared at him in surprise. "The old ways? You're joking, right? We stand for what we've always stood for … unity. Since when did it become an old way?"

Bushy cleared his throat. "Since the division broke the unity of the tribes. Since the tribes stopped trusting each other."

"I'm aware of that, but it confuses me, because this division did not take place so long ago that we now have to fight for our lives, against our own race. I also don't grasp how some keepers forgot that we cannot survive without each other."

Bushy scratched his chin. "I suppose you're right, but the grudge is too strong to avoid. The false accusations were an insult to the tribes."

Aire shook his head in dismay. "You mean to tell me that a bruised ego is enough reason to destroy the existence of all keepers. What hope is left for us if so many believe in such nonsense?"

Raine stepped forward. "I did not see any divisions in Par when I visited there a few days ago. Perhaps you are only trying to sway us to your ridiculous rebellion."

Bushy gave them a crooked smile. "No, I'm not. But I realised after Aire spoke last night, that he speaks the truth. We are destroying our race. As for Par, your observations are only partly correct. Trouble is approaching. Soon the city will be attacked. Word is out that whichever rebel group holds the city, holds authority over Equilibria. This means that all rebel groups are planning to invade the city. This is also the reason why all groups are trying to find a stronghold, should they fail to conquer the city. It's only the airlings that consider themselves strong enough to operate without a stronghold. But then again, I suppose they don't need a home if they can happily live in the air."

"What about the earthlings?" Raine asked.

Bushy shrugged his shoulders. "They were also planning on taking this outpost. They were aware that we were on our way here, but if they hear that we've failed, you can be certain they will come soon enough."

Aire lifted an eyebrow and thought for a moment. All tribes were powerful in their own right, but the earthlings and the airlings were as destructive as the aqualings. They could create havoc in no time. Yet, without unity, they were not unbeatable. Known as tough warriors and excellent with weaponry, he did not look forward to a battle with the earthlings. Besides, last night was hard on the females and his original plan had been to avoid the loss of lives.

Raine stood like a sculpture with folded arms in front of the cages. He was watching the captives suspiciously. "Where are the earthlings now?"

"We saw them setting up camp halfway between here and the western outpost. I suspect that they will either come here or try to take the western outpost from the woodlings," said Bushy.

Aire smiled and flashed a pair of straight white teeth. "Ah ha, I see. Thank you for your co-operation fellow keepers."

Bushy frowned at him. "Does this mean you will release us?" he asked.

"No, not until I am sure that you don't plan to slit our throats. For now, you may remain here as our guests."

Bushy looked down and mumbled, "Guests in cages."

"I heard that," Aire's voice rumbled. Then he flashed them another smile. "We will construct a bigger, more comfortable cage and feed you well. Consider it a resting holiday."

After taking care of the prisoners, Aire called his team together. He moved with absolute power as he walked towards the centre of their meeting place. Before he could address them, Muddy blurted out, "Is that it? No ruffing them up a bit?"

Shadow looked amused by Muddy's question. The earthling still had some fight left in him. Aire frowned at Muddy. "Why do you want to ruff them up when we've got the information we need?"

Muddy blew a red strand of hair out of his eyes. "Ah, just because …"

Aire shook his head and cut him short. "Don't get too greedy for battle my friend, there might just be more to come."

Muddy lowered his head in disappointment. He had been looking forward to the interrogation and felt cheated by the rather easy way the plantlings had imparted information.

Aire cleared his throat and his firm expression hardened. "Light Bearers, you've all heard what Bushy had to say. I am afraid he is telling the truth. I don't want another attack on our dwelling. We must come up with a diversion."

Raine watched him doubtfully. "How can you believe that rogue? He might be lying just to save himself."

"Bushy is cunning, but he has come too close to death to lie to us and he lost a warrior." Aire's eyes briefly found Lilly's as if to, once again, assure her that her actions had not been without honour. "Besides, what he said made perfect sense." He paused a few moments as if he was about to reveal a big secret. "It's what I would have done if I were them."

Raine nodded in agreement. He accepted his commander's judgment, not because he trusted the plantlings, but because he trusted Aire more than he trusted anyone. He would willingly put his life into this airling's hands, knowing that Aire would always choose his life above his own.

Aire smiled and he slapped Raine on his shoulder in a brotherly way. He understood Raine's choice to trust him completely.

"You honour me greatly, my friend," he said. He had not expected anything less, but it still gave him a warm fuzzy feeling. When he had come up with the idea of the Light Bearers, he had only considered purpose. He never once imagined how the bonds would affect him. These keepers surrounding him now were more important than anything else. *I will not put their lives in unnecessary danger*, he told himself.

"We need to focus on the next step. If we are constantly defending our outpost, we will grow weaker. I think the best thing to do is to make the earthlings believe that the plantlings succeeded in their quest and in doing so, discourage them from coming here. We just need to figure out how."

Lilly's big eyes grew even bigger as she said, "I am a plantling, perhaps they will believe me if I go to them and tell them so."

Aire shook his head. "No Lilly, your innocence shines bright like the midday sun. They will never believe you. Instead, you will end up as their prisoner."

Muddy stepped forward. "I will go. They won't frown upon my presence. I'll tell them that the plantlings took over our outpost and that I am left without a home. That could serve as the reason why I want to join their rebellion. I am sure they won't mind another member."

Aire rubbed his chin. "Are you sure about this? It sounds like a good plan, but I don't want to put your life in danger."

"Have faith in me, chief," Muddy answered cheerfully, using Maple's pet name for Aire. This broke the wall of seriousness and everyone laughed at his endearment.

From under his hood, Shadow quirked a brow and his deep voice vibrated as he spoke. "If Muddy does succeed and they do believe that the plantlings hold the post, what stops them from coming here to take the post from the plantlings?"

Aire's eyes sparkled with humour. "Shadow, you sure are a fine strategist. You always think ten steps ahead. I doubt that they would do it for exactly the same reason that I don't want us involved in another fight. It would weaken their strength and their real goal is to take the city. I also suspect that with the other rebel groups having their eyes on the same goal, time is of great importance. They wouldn't want to lose the prize to another rebel group. No, I'm sure they would rather travel through the forest and use it to their advantage, than continuously try and gain a temporary stronghold."

Shadow relaxed. A smile lurked at the edges of his mouth. He did not care much for praises, but their commander just called him a fine strategist, and that was something to be proud of.

"Muddy, I'd prefer to keep you from danger," Aire said, turning back to the earthling, "but I think this is our best option."

Muddy rubbed his two hands together. "Does this mean you will allow me to go?"

Aire laughed and shook his head. "Eager to get killed, my friend?"

A slow smile formed at Muddy's mouth. "No chief, eager to defend our fortress."

Aire returned a knowing grin. "If you insist, how can I deny you? Yes, you may go, but only under certain conditions."

Muddy frowned.

"Your first priority is to stay alive. Then I need you to convince them that the plantlings succeeded in their quest and lastly you need to find out when they plan to invade the city. This will also give us an indication of what the other rebel groups are planning. I'm certain that the earthlings have their own spies. Do I make myself clear?"

Muddy inhaled deeply before answering. "Yes, chief."

Then he looked around at his fellow warriors and said, "I will not fail you. Perhaps you fear that I will join their rebellion and not return, but only the Light Bearers have my allegiance now."

Raine surprised everyone and revealed his emotions by throwing his strong arms around Muddy in a brotherly embrace. "We never doubted you for a second. Of course you would never betray us, you are one of us."

Muddy was overtaken by the earnest affection and his eyes grew slightly wet, but he quickly stood up straight as if to remind himself that he was a warrior and that sentiments should be kept at a distance. "Wow, hang on there, buddy! Perhaps being mated makes a male soft," he teased.

Laughter erupted and everyone hugged him and spoke kind words of affection and assurance. Nobody liked the idea of their brother placing himself in the camp of the enemy, but all agreed that it was by far the best strategy.

Just as Muddy was about to leave, Lilly grabbed his arm. She held out a small pouch to him.

"What is this?"

Lilly opened the pouch and retrieved a beautiful green leaf with silver veins on it. "This is a leaf from the Triumph Bush. It's the symbol of victory amongst the plantlings. Take it with you. You might need it."

Muddy smiled. He didn't exactly believe in all the superstitions and healing herbs of the plantlings, but he didn't want to insult his friend. He gave her a quick peck on the cheek and slipped the pouch into his pocket. Then he waved goodbye and followed the footpath to the west.

Aire, normally always in control, found it difficult to swallow the lump that formed in his throat. He wished this division had never happened. He wished things could just go back to the way they used to be. He hoped that his brother would be safe.

Chapter 15

As Muddy strolled along, he remembered the words that Aire had spoken earlier. It was strange to be called brave, but he liked it. *I sure hope I'm brave*, he said to himself. Suddenly, his eyes widened in surprise as a dagger flew past his head. Without thinking, he threw himself on the ground and rolled in the sand. The sand particles, being elemental to his nature, covered him and served as a good camouflage. In the blink of an eye, he became almost invisible.

Muddy's heart was pounding in his ears as he tried to get his breathing under control. He lay flat on his stomach and squinted to see where his attacker was. He heard whispers and approaching footsteps. From the slight vibrations in the ground, he determined that there were at least two of them and sure enough, they emerged from behind a big tree on his left. *Earthlings? Trying to kill me and I am one of them. How disturbing. They have no loyalty to their own kind. They've just become my enemy.*

As they drew closer, Muddy decided that he probably needed to impress them if he wanted acceptance into their rebel group. He waited till they were just a short distance away and then he spread his hands out, flat on the earth, making slow circles with them. The ground trembled and cracks appeared everywhere. The two rogues struggled to stay upright. One of them shouted, "Show yourself!"

Muddy ignored them and continued to gently coax the ground, singing a soft earth tune. The earth shook more violently and the two fell down hard. One nearly fell into a crack.

"Stop, please stop! We are earthlings," the other one shouted.

Muddy slowly brought his hands to rest and the earth calmed down. He got up and dusted himself off as his bright amber eyes found theirs.

"Did you eat too much dust?" he teased and then his eyes turned emotionless. "You are earthlings like me, yet you attacked me. Why?"

"We were not sure what you were, since your clothes are rather plain compared to the rest of our kind," one with light-brown hair answered.

Muddy nearly blurted out, "Liars," but he managed to swallow the words in time. "You mean to say, just because I choose not to wear gemstones on my clothing like you, I don't qualify as an earthling? Or is it because my hair is red?" Muddy tried his best to sound as playful as possible.

The one with dark-grey hair stared at him distrustfully. "You obviously are one. You even know how to charm the earth; a valuable skill, not mastered by all earthlings," he countered with sarcasm dripping from his lips.

Muddy took a moment to let his gaze drift over the earthlings, noticing a number of daggers hanging from their belts. He smiled cunningly at them. "Yup, I'm one of the few who can, but you two are skilled in the craftsmanship of weaponry."

The brown-haired one lifted an eyebrow. "Yes, indeed we are. Tell me, where are you off to?"

"Perhaps fellow earthlings, it's more appropriate to get acquainted first," he said, bowing low before them in a gallant manner. "I'm Muddy, son of Clay, and who are you?"

The two earthlings looked at each other and back at Muddy again, then the brown-haired one placed a hand on his chest saying, "I'm Pebble and this is Gravel," gesturing towards his friend. "Now tell us where you are headed."

Muddy contemplated his answer. *Very interested in my whereabouts, aren't we?* Aloud he said, "I am heading further west, looking for rebels."

The two looked at him intensely. *Now I've got your attention.*

"What would your reason be?" Gravel nearly groaned.

Muddy kept them in suspense for a few moments as he narrowed his eyes and rubbed his chin. "The plantlings took over our southern outpost and killed most of my team. I escaped, but not before I heard them say that an earthling rebel group is west of here. I want to join them, since I am now homeless and fairly angry at the plantlings. What about you two, do you want to join me?"

They ignored his question, looking at each other with uncertainty. Pebble returned his gaze to Muddy and looked him up and down. Muddy could read the doubt in his eyes.

"Why not go back to Par?" Pebble finally asked.

Muddy smiled again, but this time he gave a cruel twist to his mouth, to convince them that he had nothing but payback on his mind. "There's nothing left for me amongst the fineries in Par. I want revenge. I didn't plan to be part of this division, but now the plantlings leave me with no other choice. Besides I've heard that no one in Par takes the situation seriously and the elders pretend that nothing is amiss." Muddy saw the softening in the eyes of his rivals and he knew that he had just won them over.

Gravel stepped forward and grasped Muddy's forearms, as was the customary greeting of warriors, and a sign of respect. "Well Muddy, son of Clay, seek no more. You've found your brethren. Come with us to our commander, Soil, and state your case. I think he would be pleased to hear that we've found a ground whisperer."

They travelled further west and, after a while, reached a camp. Upon entering, inquisitive faces peered at them and soon Muddy was surrounded by more of his kind.

"What is causing the fuss?" he heard a voice rumbling behind him. He turned around and found himself staring into the eyes of Soil, the rebel commander of the earthlings. Soil was a handsome male, but his deep brown eyes held only shadow, giving Muddy the impression of dark pits.

Gravel quickly stepped forward and said, "We found him wandering not far from here. He is a ground whisperer."

Soil looked at him without blinking an eye. Muddy could almost feel the warrior sizing him up. The rebel commander's expression held toughness and Muddy's palms rapidly became sweaty. Gravel saved him by doing introductions. All Muddy's frozen state allowed him to do in response was nod his head. Pebble, the more fluent one, explained in fine detail Muddy's previous display of power and about his desire to join them. Everyone seemed happy to welcome him, except for Soil, who still gazed at him suspiciously.

After a few moments of noise and chaos, Soil lifted his hand. "Silence!"

Stillness fell upon the group and stretched for a few long moments before he spoke again. He looked Muddy straight in the eye. "I will not question your reasons for being here, son of Clay, but know this, if I find them treacherous, you will die a slow and painful death."

Muddy felt his blood run cold. The mark of the Light Bearers was beginning to glow and he quickly placed his hand in his pocket to hide it. Sweat gathered on his brow and he had to pull on all his reserves in order to appear calm. Nodding slowly, he said, "Yes sir, understood."

Then Soil turned around and walked away.

That evening, the earthlings gathered around a campfire. They shared a meal and made jokes about the other unfortunate tribes. The earthlings were confident that with their skills of weaponry, gemstone calling and ground whispering, they would be the most likely tribe to win the upcoming war. Once they succeeded in taking over the city of Par, they would be the leaders of Equilibria.

Muddy sat quietly, resting his elbows on his knees and listening to their conversation. He sat in the shadows to avoid drawing too much attention to himself. One of them asked, "What will we do with the tribe elder, Quake, once we have taken Par?"

Soil took a long sip from his goblet, as if he was savouring the taste of his drink, and then he laughed mockingly. "Ha! We will throw him in a dungeon with the rest of the elders. He deserves no better – he has forsaken his tribe."

Everyone joined in mocking laughter and soon after Soil got up and announced that he was retiring for the evening. His absence gave Muddy a bit more courage and after a while, he cleared his throat. "Why are you so certain that our skills are superior?"

Gravel gave him an irritated look. "You have little faith. We are expert weapon masters. We are one with the metals in the mountains, we can call any gemstone from its hidden place. How many tribes have the control over and riches of gemstones? And of course, now we have a ground whisperer. You can create mayhem amongst our enemies with your tricks. So, yes I believe we are unmatched and that victory is ours for the taking." He gave the others a huge smile, revealing perfect front teeth.

Muddy tossed Gravel a disinterested glance and fiddled with his pointy ears. After a few moments he interrupted the talk of war again and asked innocently, "Do you actually believe that a war is possible? Sure, there have been fights amongst the different tribes, but war would involve all the tribes fighting against each other. No offence, but it sounds a bit far-fetched to me. I can accept battles, but a war?" Shaking his head, he made a "tsk" sound with his tongue, as if to dismiss the idea completely.

Big eyes stared at him in disbelief. *They've taken the bait,* he realised. Gravel grew red in his face. He stood up and towered over Muddy. "How dare you insult us like this? You are foolish. Of course a war will take place. It's inevitable. As a matter of fact, it is considered that once Par has been taken, the rest of the tribes will challenge each other. That's why we have to move quickly. In two risings we will take the city and claim our rule. With the earthlings as rulers, we will hold the most power and wealth. Who can conquer such a kingdom?"

Cheers went up from the crowd as they all banged their blades against each others' in a display of power.

You ignorant fools, the words popped into Muddy's mind. He suddenly felt sick. Their conviction was troubling. He had to get this information to Aire as soon as possible. His mindless tribe mates were stubborn and determined, regardless of the cost to their lives or the lives of others. How arrogant of them to think that power and wealth could shield them from attack. Had they forgotten how destructive the aqualings and the airlings were? Neither metal weapons nor pretty coloured stones would be able to stop them.

Muddy fell into silence and listened to the others brag about their skills. He gave them enough time to indulge themselves in their pride and to forget about him, before he decided to take his leave. He scooped up two handfuls of sand from the ground and slipped this quietly into his pockets, his fingers finding the pouch he had received from Lilly. He smiled. *Perhaps the superstitious gift will be useful after all*, he thought.

Giving a willful yawn, he got up and excused himself, claiming that he was tired as he slipped away sheepishly to a nearby tree. Near its base was a small chamber that would make a good shelter. He crawled into it and waited for the others to retire.

Chapter 16

When the moon was high, Muddy picked up a sharp stone and cut his palm open. Then he tore off a piece of his shirt and wrapped it around the wound to soak up the blood. Lilly's Triumph Bush leaf came in handy and he placed it neatly on his resting place. He waited a while before removing the blood-soaked cloth and positioned it with the leaf, covering both items with a flat stone to hold them down. He hoped that they would create the impression that he had been abducted by plantlings. If the earthlings believed this, the symbol would send a clear message to them. Hopefully something like, *Stay away! We can get to you anytime we want to.*

Slowly he removed the sand from his pockets and rubbed it all over him. He expected a good coverage that would not betray his position when he crawled out of the hole. Sailing on his belly, he stayed close to the ground, all the while rubbing more sand on him. Soon he was camouflaged and moved with ease. There were three guards in the vicinity, but he easily slipped past them unnoticed. When he reached the edge of the camp, he stood and took off at a rapid pace, running as fast as he could. His chest was burning like fire but he kept going.

He was still moving fast when something tripped him and he fell down hard. When he looked up, he stared into the eyes of a guard. The attack happened so fast; Muddy had barely time to register what was happening. He was still trying to get up when the guard lifted a blade and swung it at him. Muddy scrambled back and jumped to his feet. The rogue charged forward and as Muddy moved to evade him, he lost his footing again.

The rebel guard lifted his blade to deal a deathblow. Muddy knew it was now or never. He rolled towards his opponent and knocked him over with a hard jolt to the knee. When he sagged, Muddy took the opportunity and grabbed the hand in which he held the blade. They rolled and wrestled on the ground. His opponent attempted to alarm the rest of the earthlings, but Muddy smothered the sound with a bunch of leaves that he grabbed from a nearby tree. As he stuffed them into his rival's mouth, his opponent nearly slit his throat. Muddy finally had the upper hand and thrust the blade into his opponent's neck, killing him instantly. Relief flooded over him as the rogue's body went limp.

As Muddy looked into the dead eyes of his fellow earthling, great remorse filled him. His sorrow increased even more as he watched the dramatic display of the corpse turning into a heap of dust. Death for any keeper meant the return of a once glorious body to its elemental form. For a few moments he was lost, before he realised that his fingers still clenched the bloody blade. He threw it down as though it had burned him and stared at his fingers. He shook uncontrollably and tried to control his body by hugging it tightly. He realised how Lilly must have felt after she had killed one of her own kind. Once again, the situation replayed itself. It was either his life or the life of the rebel. Oh, how he hated the division and this rebellion. It was wrong, everything was wrong.

A trail of trickling blood caught his attention, and he inspected his throbbing leg. He rapidly scooped up a handful of sand, rubbed it into the wound, and limped away. Countless times he found himself wondering how he, a life giver, had ended up being an agent of death. His blood must have turned to ice, because he couldn't stop trembling.

After he had travelled a short distance, he peeked over his shoulder to see if he was being followed. It didn't seem likely. He relaxed a bit, but increased his speed, wanting to get away before

Soil could get his hands on him. The thought of the commander's threat tightened Muddy's chest a little more.

Muddy hoped that the fake warning he left behind – the bloodied knife and the heap of dust – would convince the earthlings that he had been abducted. If they didn't believe it, he would be a marked target and be killed without hesitation. Perhaps he should have stayed longer. He wondered if he would be able to talk his way out of the dilemma if they succeeded in capturing him. Shaking his head, he answered himself, *Nah Muddy, you're as good as dead.*

Pressing on in an eerie silence, he mourned the death of his earthling brother. He wanted to condemn himself for the deed, but no matter how many times he replayed his actions over and over in his mind, he couldn't. Another possible scenario struck him. If he had hesitated, he would be the one whose blood would have coloured the forest floor. There had been no other option. What was happening to Equilibria? Evil had swept through their once beautiful forest. How much more did they have to endure of these perilous times?

Look on the bright side, if the Light Bearers fail in their quest to stop the war, then everyone will die. He got irritated with his own thoughts. *Gloom and doom! Pull yourself together, Muddy. You're still alive and you've got a duty of light and honour to fulfill.*

Muddy approached their outpost and was immediately relieved. The past few hours had been unbearable and he was glad to be home. He hated feeling like a coward, but he couldn't help the anxiousness that nipped at him. He had been afraid that the rebels would follow him and kill him. His shoulders sagged as he walked into their holding. He was exhausted.

A twig snapped and then a hand crossed his mouth as a blade pressed against his neck. His spine stiffened. *No! I've led them home,* was his first thought, but then he heard Shadow's familiar deep voice next to his ear. "You walk unguarded brother. We have enemies now; you cannot just stroll into our outpost without being alert."

Muddy sighed in relief. "Shadow, thank goodness it's you and not them."

Shadow let him go and stepped in front of him. He lifted his eyebrow and stared at Muddy. "Explain."

"Let's first gather the others," Muddy replied in a haunted voice.

Shadow mimicked the squawk of a raven and the other keepers appeared out of nowhere. Muddy frowned.

"What's up with all the snooping?" he asked as his friends approached.

Raine was the first to greet him with a hug and the rest followed his example. Aire stepped forward and placed a hand on Muddy's shoulder. "Glad to have you back. We have to be watchful now. We don't know who might be a friend or a foe. Why are you back so soon? Did you come across trouble?"

Muddy looked around again, as if to ensure that he had not been followed. "Trouble, indeed."

Aire crossed his arms and his strong muscles flexed. "What kind of trouble?"

Muddy looked at his friends' worried faces. He told them about the rebels' plans, as well as his escape. He shared his fears that his hoax might be a complete failure and his hopes that the rebels would believe the deception, that of his supposed abduction.

Then, of course, there was the issue of the dead guard. Muddy's colouring turned an odd pale bronze when he told them about the earthling he had killed. He swallowed hard as he looked down at his fingers again. Aire squeezed his shoulder in understanding and Shadow slapped him a few times gently on his back in comradeship.

"Do you think they will come after me?" he asked Aire.

The commander rubbed his chin. "I really don't know. I doubt Soil would risk the lives of his loyal followers to retrieve an earthling whom he didn't know or trust. You also don't know the exact details of his plans. However, the fact that they lost a guard and a ground whisperer might be an irritating thorn in his side. I cannot say for sure if he will come for you, but you must all stay alert in case he does."

Shadow heard the subtle undertone of his commander's warning and frowned at him. "What do you mean all of us? What about you?"

Aire shook his head and smiled. "Shadow, you're becoming as sharp as that bird of prey you keep company with. You picked that up, huh? Well, you're right. I will be off to Par in the morning."

Raine stepped forward. "Par! What are you going to do there? We need you here to lead us."

Aire's eyes found Raine's.

"I am going to do what must be done. I must warn the elders that Par will soon be attacked. Besides, you are more than capable leading the team in my absence."

Raine's eyes nearly popped out. "Who … me? But …"

Aire interrupted him. "Yes. You, Raine! As from this moment forth, you are my second-in-command."

Raine's questioning gaze found Aire. "You've never chosen a second before. Why now? You don't have any plans of dying on us, do you?" Gasps went up from Dew and Lilly.

Maple pointed a finger at Raine and lifted her chin. "Raine, stop being an oaf! You can be as blunt as Shadow sometimes."

He gave her an irritated look and returned his gaze to Aire. She shook her head, as Shadow flashed his white teeth and poked his tongue at her. A snort escaped from Maple and a tear slipped down Lilly's pale face.

"Lilly! Why do you always have to cry about everything? We are facing troubling times; please pull yourself together." Realising that she might get in trouble, she smiled sweetly at Lilly and patted her lightly on her shoulder.

Lilly was visibly annoyed and arched an eyebrow at Maple. She placed a hand on her hip and looked as if she was provoking Maple when she said, "My crying is not a sign of weakness, Maple. It is a sign of compassion. Just in case you forgot, I am quite capable of defending myself in these perilous times we find ourselves in. The dry remains of another plantling are proof of that."

Everyone stared at Lilly in disbelief and Maple went red in her face. She was as shocked as the rest. To save some of her dignity she responded, "My, oh my, you've finally learned to stand up for yourself. Well done, sister."

"Enough!" Aire's voice thundered. "Raine, I have no intention of dying, but we also have never faced a threat of extinction before. You will lead the team in my absence and that's a command." He looked back at everyone. "As for the rest of you, you will respect Raine's leadership and do as he says. Oh, and Maple, also remember to respect the rest of your fellow Light Bearers."

Everyone's heads lowered. No one wanted to look into Aire's now darkened eyes.

The only one bold enough to ask a question was Shadow. He stood broad-shouldered and cleared his throat. "What happens if the elders reject our course of action?"

Aire's face was stricken with concern as he shook his head in uncertainty. "If that happens, we will need to make a choice between our loyalty to the elders and the survival of our race. I hope it won't come to that," he said, his words leaving a bitter taste on his tongue.

"What if something happens to the rest of us while you're gone?" Muddy wanted to know.

Aire shrugged his shoulders. "Raine will know what to do."

An unearthly silence fell over the team.

As Aire turned and walked away from them, he said, "If you don't hear from me in two risings, then you must assume that I did not make it."

Chapter 17

The next day, after surfing on the wind, Aire found himself looking down on the city of Par. The aerial view of it was spectacular. He could see the big Oak Tree with its looming presence in front of Mount Dashar. Its branches thick and covered with the green growth of new leaves. Surrounding it were more trees, which held many dwellings. To add to its splendor was the creek that flowed through it and the many rocks and flowers that surrounded it. *Ah, it is always a sight to behold*, he thought.

Normally he would go straight to the palace inside the big Oak. Once in the great hall, he would enter by the door that led to the cave entrance inside the mountain. A tunnel would then take him to the Sacred Chamber for the council meetings. He frowned as he took in his surroundings and stepped down from the wave of air he had travelled on. Everything seemed at peace. He received some curious glances and a few nods, but nothing out of the ordinary.

On his way to the palace, he passed a lovely female from his tribe, who introduced herself as Skye. He greeted her and had the most compelling impulse to share a few words. She was struggling to carry some pitchers and Aire automatically took two to help her with her load. They chatted a bit more about the weather and nonessential things until they reached a chamber where more females were entering and leaving. None of them seemed the least bit interested in the two of them, since the feast of Solace was over and no one would conclude that they might be a new pair. They were just two airlings having a conversation.

"Could you perhaps tell me where I can find the tribe elders?" Aire asked as they entered the chamber. She gave him a friendly smile and gestured towards the ancient Oak.

"The sun must be shining special rays on you today, Aire. Even as we speak, they gather in the great hall. Perhaps you should join them for their midday meal."

Aire couldn't help but stare at her as he held her words captive. *Midday meal! It must be nice to have midday meals. At the outpost, we only have enough to break our fast in the morning and quiet the worst of the hunger pains at night.* She looked at him with big grey eyes. "Did I say something wrong?"

He realised that she was taken aback by his silence. "Pardon, no you did not. A thought just crossed my mind, that's all." He thanked her and walked on as she uttered a delayed appreciation after him.

As he entered the great hall, he was even more surprised by its fineries. The tables were lavishly decorated. The sounds of lyre and flutes travelled over the hall and the aroma of delicious food filled the air. He experienced weakness to his stomach as the scents of lavender and pine combined with fresh fruit burned in his nostrils. It was all too exquisite for an outpost keeper like himself and deep down his inner voice told him that he did not fit in Par anymore. The table of the elders was at the far northern end on a raised platform, clearly indicating their seats of honour. Four guards stopped him as he approached.

"Let him pass," he heard the booming voice of his tribe elder, Cyclone. It travelled unhindered through the great hall. Aire sized up the guards and reckoned that he could easily take them out. *Even their guards have become refined. These fools will not be able to defend the city*, he thought.

"What brings you here Aire, son of Atmos? It is not yet time for a council meeting," the elder stated arrogantly.

Aire stood before the six elders and wondered how detached they really were from the rest of the keepers, since they seemed unaffected about the last council meeting, disaster that it was. They looked impressive and frightening at the same time with glorious robes flowing from their shoulders.

"I seek the council of the tribe elders. I have some disturbing news to share."

Everyone knew that Cyclone was short-tempered and unpredictable. This left Aire a little uncomfortable as the tribe elder's stormy eyes bored into him. "Well then, join our table and share your information with us," he said, without blinking an eye.

Aire was an impressive force on his own, but knew that he stood in the dragon's lair, surrounded by the most ferocious and powerful keepers. Although they showed him hospitality, he could feel that they were not too pleased with his presence. He suddenly doubted his sense in coming.

He held on to every nerve as he told them of the rebel groups' plans to attack. Quake, the knowledgeable elder of the earthlings, pulled on his little goatee beard and his diamond-coloured eyes grew dark as he looked at Aire. "How did you get this information?' he finally asked. *Here it is now. The moment of truth has arrived*, Aire thought.

He looked at them, back and forth, and pulled his hand through his pearl white hair.

Ivy, elder of the plantlings, moved her wrist and rolled her hand in front of her as she spoke. "Go on." He looked at her ethereal beauty and wondered how such a vision of a female could hold a seat amongst the most powerful keeper males. Then he remembered that she was equally powerful and that her beauty was probably just another weapon.

Aire sighed. He began by telling them about the formation of the Light Bearers, keeping his eyes fixed on the table as he spoke. When he finally finished, he looked up and found Tsunami, the aggressive elder of the aqualings, rising out of his chair.

The sound of crashing waves filled the hall, as he thundered, "You did what?"

Griffin, the powerful, roared like a big cat and said, "Och, sit down Tsunami. Your display does not impress anyone, except for him perhaps. Tell us what your so-called Light Bearers have discovered on their quests."

Tsunami took his seat again. Aire slowly continued to give an account of the discoveries the spies had made, but he kept a watchful eye on Tsunami. It was when he told them about the attack of the rebel plantlings, that he could sense strong emotions being projected towards him. When he finally looked up again, Ivy just stared at him in disbelief.

"What did you do with the prisoners?" Aire fixed his eyes on her. Her pale green skin was flustered with a deep purple blush. She was upset.

"We made them a comfortable cage, my lady. My team takes good care of them and they are not hostile anymore. However, we cannot release them yet, as we are not sure if we can trust them not to partake in the planned overthrow of leadership."

Cyclone's colour had changed into that of a charged lightning bolt. *By all that is sacred, the tribe elder looks like he wants to strike me dead on the spot*, Aire realised. Maybe coming here was a bad idea after all.

"Your father, Atmos, would have killed you himself," Cyclone exclaimed, as if he knew what his thoughts were.

Aire could see that the tribe elder was barely keeping a leash on his powers and then Cyclone rose from his seat, with Tsunami following his action. Cyclone clutched his fists and Tsunami pressed his palms down hard on the table. The sound of thunder rolled through the air and lightning bolts formed above the table. Tsunami joined in the dreadful display with the sound of rushing water and crashing waves, as fog formed all around him. Aire experienced déjà vu as he recalled their last unsuccessful council meeting, when the elders also displayed their intimidating powers. They were furious.

Quake held up his hand in an attempt to restore order to the charged atmosphere. "Sit down, both of you. What do you want to do, bring down the walls on us? This is no way to take charge of a situation and you know it."

The other two elders did not seem in a hurry to calm down, but they did manage to control their fury somewhat.

"His offence is great. What will we do with him?" he heard a gruff voice say from across the table. He turned his head and stared into the eyes of Thekku, elder of the woodlings. He had been so silent throughout the briefing that Aire had completely forgotten about him.

"Lock him up until we've reached a decision. We will deliver judgment in the morning," Cyclone said.

Thekku was not pleased with the answer. "No, I say we banish him and his foolish followers," he countered, his voice rising another octave. Aire turned cold at the judgment and tiny dust specks moved at high speed around him. He was offended. He found the odd emotions flowing through him disturbing. He had to calm down before he acted irrationally and jeopardised the plans of the Light Bearers. Thankful for his many years of discipline and training, he concentrated on his breathing and forced himself to remain still. Discipline was the only thing to rely on at that moment, perhaps the only thing that would keep him alive.

Quake raised an eyebrow at the woodling's remark. "Thekku, you know very well that is not the way we deal with offences. We will hold a hearing, as we've always done," he challenged with flashing eyes.

Thekku eyed the earthling tribe elder and then shifted his gaze to Aire. "Very well, let the morning come soon then," he mocked and his humourless chuckle left Aire hopeless.

The rest of them dipped their heads in agreement and Cyclone motioned for the guards to take Aire away. "Put him in a secure holding chamber," he demanded.

Griffin said, "Tsk," as he shook his head. "It's a sad day Aire, that you should be our prisoner and not our guest. We've always held you with great regard. Take care of his needs," Griffin instructed as Aire was guided out of the great hall.

Aire didn't resist. His mind travelled to his team. With him being locked up, how would they know that the egotistical elders rejected his information?

"So much for trying to warn them," Aire mumbled to himself. For a brief moment he wondered whether he should escape, but decided against it. He didn't want to lead them to his friends or suffer unnecessary wounds, especially not with a war so close. He frowned as he realised that should he attempt to escape, Cyclone would not hesitate to strike him dead.

As they dragged him along a footpath to the entrance of a nearby tree, they passed Skye. Her face was expressionless as she watched him. Aire found it rather strange that she was not moved by his humiliating experience. It did not happen often amongst their race that someone was arrested or dragged through the city like a lawless fool. After seeing the distressed glances of the other bystanders, he concluded that perhaps Skye was just strong. The embarrassment that he experienced at that moment was beyond what he could bear. He lowered his head and hoped that they would pass her quickly.

Chapter 18

A ire found himself standing in the centre of an underground holding chamber. A wooden door covered the entrance of the small, stuffy room.

Aire studied his new surroundings and saw a small pallet of straw to rest on, against the back wall. In the far corner was a cup filled with water. The walls were plastered with hardened clay and thick roots from the tree above covered them in a network of veins. He took a few strides and plopped down onto the pallet. Lying on his back, he put his arms under his head and stared at the door.

He must have fallen asleep, because the opening of the chamber door startled him. He looked up into the big grey eyes of Skye.

"Pardon me, did I wake you?" she asked, smiling nervously at him.

"No," he replied in a voice he did not recognise as his own. He was shocked to see her.

"I've brought you some food," she said uneasily.

From a basket, she took a plate of delicious fruits and nuts. At once, his stomach rumbled and he sat up quickly. Skye smiled at the sound of it and placed the plate neatly down next to him. Aire gave her a thankful smile as he reached for it.

"I thought you shared a meal at midday with the elders?" she asked.

He shook his head as he devoured the food. She had no idea how uncomfortable the meeting with the elders had been. Food had been the last thing on his mind. She stood watching him for a while and then passed a cup to him. Aire easily recalled the high quality honey bush tea from the previous council meeting, only this cup tasted sweeter than ever. He continued to eat without paying any attention to her, but looked up as she turned and walked towards the door.

"Wait, please wait," he stumbled over his words.

She stopped and looked at him over her shoulder.

"Please sit with me. I could do with some company."

Skye looked uncertain, but turned around and sat next to him. He relaxed and wiped his mouth with the back of his hand. He figured he might as well see what he could learn.

"What time of the day is it?"

"Three hours before sunset," she replied softly. She did not look at him and kept her eyes fixed on the floor.

He looked at her profile and noticed how delicate her features were. Thick black lashes framed her grey eyes and her skin looked velvety soft. She wore her long silver hair in a braid that fell over her shoulder. Skye was pretty, not as beautiful as many other females in his tribe, yet there was something that set her apart. She carried herself like a princess but at the same time was as humble as a servant. Aire frowned and two small lines formed between his eyebrows.

He suddenly wondered why he had never considered taking a lifemate before. Aire pushed the unlikely thought quickly out of his mind when his eye caught the chamber door behind her. It reminded him why he was in prison in the first place. He was not a lovesick fool like Raine. No, he had responsibilities.

Skye peeked at him shyly from under her lashes. "Why are you in here?" she asked.

He stared at her for a moment and then his defences crumbled. For some inexplicable reason, he wanted her to know the truth. He told her everything and when he was done, waited for her reaction. Whatever he expected, he was surprised.

She looked at him and said, "You're very brave."

Aire was dumbstruck and humbled at the same time. No judgment – in its place just one sentence that praised him. She confused him.

"What about you? I know your name, but who are you and why do you serve me?" he wanted to know.

"I am Skye, daughter of Cyclone. Nobody wanted to come down here and bring you nourishment, so I volunteered."

Aire could not believe his ears. She was the daughter of his tribe elder, which meant that she was a princess. And yet she was serving him by choice. What was she really doing there? Was she a spy for Cyclone?

"Your father must be upset that you came down here. You do realise that they consider me dangerous. Why did you come?"

"I don't think you're dangerous," she said with a puzzled look on her face. "You've only been kind to me. Anyway, my father must deal with his own anger and he cannot hold me responsible for his failures."

Aire's eyes grew wide in disbelief and shock. She was the only one he knew who was not afraid of Cyclone.

"What failures?" he asked, trying to see if she would reveal anything more.

"The elders have failed the race of the keepers," she answered flatly.

Aire lifted an eyebrow as he realised that Skye was definitely not doing Cyclone's bidding. "Exactly how have they done that?"

Her eyes grew big like two large grey thunderclouds, and he detected anger when she spoke. "They are too comfortable in their lovely surroundings, while other keepers struggle daily to survive in the forest. In their arrogance and power, they have forgotten that they are not just elders, but caretakers too."

"Do you find me too outspoken?" she suddenly asked, narrowing her eyes suspiciously.

"No, not at all," he laughed. "I like your directness and you speak with wisdom. But it does strike me as odd that a princess does not support her father."

"Please do not refer to me as a princess," she said, fiddling with her hands in her lap. Then she paused and looked him straight in the eyes. "My father disappointed me. After I was born, my mother died and a breath of wind took her remains away. He gave me to a nursemaid and did not pay much attention to me afterwards. Instead, he took another mate at the following feast of Solace."

Aire understood. Skye experienced rejection and that was why she could identify it easily in the lives of others.

"I understand your reasoning, but why reject your birthright?" he asked.

She turned her head slightly, in an almost arrogant stance. "Should I be proud of living an exalted life while my brethren struggle to survive?"

Aire looked at her in wonder and realised that he had just found an unexpected ally in Par. He took her hands in his. For a moment, his own action stunned him. She looked down at their joined hands and froze. Aire awkwardly withdrew his hands.

"Do I have your friendship, Skye?" he asked her softly.

She looked him in the eyes and whispered, "Yes you do, Aire."

Relief flooded over him and he slowly exhaled. Then he asked her to send a message to the Light Bearers, to inform them of his capture and the judgment that would take place the following morning. Skye agreed and they discussed possible ways for her to achieve this. She could travel to the Light Bearers but with the threat of an invasion, it was too dangerous for her to leave Par alone. The only other option was for her to seek the assistance of flying insects, as the tribe elders did. They decided that the best way to send a message would be for Skye to ask for help from the bees. There was a hive close by and she could call to the bees on the tunes of the wind. They would then take the message directly to Shadow, who would be able to decipher it. They spoke for a few more minutes until the guard opened the door. He folded his arms and cleared his throat. "It's time to leave now."

Skye gathered her basket and walked towards the exit.

"Skye, thank you – for everything," Aire called after her.

She turned and smiled at him one last time and then she was gone.

Aire decided that if they survived what lay ahead, then he would claim her as his lifemate. She was lovely, wise and a perfect match for him. A naughty smile formed at the corners of his mouth as he thought of Cyclone's fury if this were to pass. The male airling whom Cyclone despised the most becoming his daughter's mate. Aire threw himself back on the straw pallet and laughed so much that tears rolled down his face.

Chapter 19

Shadow was sitting on a branch high up in a tree, his legs hanging down. He chewed on a twig, watching his fellow brethren swim in the stream below. Argon was perched a few branches above him, keeping a watchful eye on the horizon. Soon his pet bird informed Shadow that a swarm of bees was approaching at high speed from the north.

Shadow stared into the direction. *Strange. Why would a swarm of bees come from the north and what is their hurry?* He kept his eyes on their movement and then with a quick acrobatic move, swung himself over the branch and landed with two feet on the ground. As the bees neared, he whistled a soft tune on the wind, calling to them.

"Greetings, my flying friends. I don't recognise you as members from the hives around here. What brings you here, so far away from your home?"

There was a loud buzz and some more buzzing. Shadow's olive skin paled and his eyes grew even darker.

"Wait, stop. Repeat, please," he said.

After a few more moments of interaction with the bees, he bid them farewell and called to the other Light Bearers.

"What's wrong?" Raine asked.

Shadow shifted uncomfortably from one leg to another before he answered. "It's Aire. They've arrested him."

Maple made a funny screeching sound and then said, "What! Why?"

Before Shadow could answer, Muddy shouted, "I knew it! He should not have gone. Those rigid elders never listen to reason."

"Please. Give him a chance to speak," Dew said calmly.

Raine frowned at her. It amazed him that she always managed to stay calm at all times. Muddy wanted to say something again, but Lilly placed an index finger on her lip. She blew wind through her teeth as she motioned to him to keep quiet. "Shh."

After all the interruptions, Shadow finally had the chance to speak again. "The bee captain brought a message from someone called Skye, a friend of Aire's. Apparently Aire has been arrested and there will be a trial tomorrow morning."

"We need to get eyes and ears at that trial," said Raine, dragging his hand through his wet, spiky hair. He looked directly at Shadow as he spoke.

"It's not possible," said Muddly. "They will probably hold the hearing in the Sacred Cave."

"Arrgg!" said Raine. "That is an impassable location."

Shadow smiled. "No, it isn't."

Questioning gazes rested upon him.

"How?" Raine wanted to know.

"If I tell you my friend, I would have to kill you," said Shadow, his smile growing bigger. "Just trust me when I say that I can get in and out of there unseen."

The concern on the faces of his friends harmed his pride. He threw up both his hands in a defensive manner. "Please! Now you're hurting my feelings. I am trained in stealth, you know."

"Yes, we know. It's just … they've got Aire already. We don't want you locked up as well," Muddy explained.

"I know," Shadow answered as he patted the red-head's shoulder awkwardly in affection.

The next morning, Shadow lay on his stomach, cloaked in the shadows of the Sacred Chamber, waiting patiently for the elders and his commander to arrive. He paid attention to every silhouette as his raven eyes scanned the surroundings of the large chamber.

The curving walls and ceiling were filled with crystals and various gemstones. From the ceiling, stalactites hung in various sizes and from the floor of the cave stalagmites stretched out to meet them. A few pools were carved out of rock formations and the water in them reflected the colours of the jewels in the walls. Shadow knew that the entire back wall was filled with the ancient scrolls that held the history and the laws of their kind. The scrolls were not visible; the holes they were kept in were sealed with gemstones. Every gemstone had a marking on it, to indicate which scroll was in the hole it covered.

In the centre of the Sacred Chamber was a huge round rock which served as a table with twelve smaller rocks placed around it. The walls glistened with moisture. Although a few tunnels left the hall forming a network of underground passages, keepers normally entered the cave by the palace entrance.

Shadow had easily avoided the guards at the front entrance and, by taking one of the less used tunnels, had gained access to the Sacred Chamber.

As he lay there waiting, he thought about the message the bees had delivered to him. His muscles stiffened. To think that the elders threw a respected commander in prison! It was beyond disappointing; it was troubling. Did it mean that they did not care about defeating the evil that threatened them? Shadow's head was spinning with all the unanswered questions. Impatience was not one of his traits, but he wanted answers. He called upon his discipline and waited patiently for any movement.

Time went by slowly but at last the elders began arriving and seated themselves. Then Aire was escorted in by two big earthlings. His hands were tied behind his back and they placed him on a seat opposite the round rock, facing the elders. Shadow blinked at the sight of Aire, finding it difficult to believe that his commander was being treated like a criminal.

Cyclone opened a scroll and began to read from it.

"Aire, Son of Atmos. You have done grave and unthinkable things. You formed a mixed tribe and lead them to spy and fight against their own kind. What do you have to say in your defence?"

Aire sat with pride in his seat. He lifted his chin and studied the faces of the elders. He couldn't find any compassion in their eyes, only arrogance.

"You charge me," he told them, "because I have strengthened what you have designed. It's the tribal elders of Equilibria who gave instruction for our groups to be mixed in the beginning. It was the tribal elders who trained us together since we were younglings. When we were old enough, you sent us to merciless outposts to protect our borders at all costs. Not once have any of you visited the outposts. With only each other to rely on, we've grown closer and stronger over time.

"The keepers in Par live in luxury and abundance, while those of us at the outposts fight for survival every day. Our different ways of living divided us from the keepers in Par long before this tribal division took place. Yet, you charge me for forming my own tribe? I did the only thing I could under the circumstances. I asked my members to make a covenant with each other in order to protect and strengthen the team. Do you realise we are the only outpost team that has not disbanded? None of us have joined the rebel groups that now threaten our very existence. No, the Light Bearers are doing everything we can to save the continuation of our race and our way of living."

Tsunami grew red in his face. "You blame us for your crimes? How dare you!"

Aire's eyes remained calm and midday-blue as he spoke. "I speak the facts. Your own consciences accuse you. Why do you think rebel groups formed in the first place? What did you expect? Is it not the duty of the elders to protect and care for the tribes? Perhaps your own failure contributed to this division."

Shadow held his breath at the statement of his commander. *Oh, this could be trouble.* He looked at the guards and the tribe elders and tried to calculate if there was any way that he could reduce their numbers in a matter of seconds, just in case he needed to save Aire's life. It seemed as though his commander had some kind of a death wish, tempting the elders in this way.

Disorder erupted as Tsunami, Cyclone and Thekku leapt up angrily.

"Sit down and control yourselves," boomed the voice of Quake, reverberating around the chamber. "This young keeper speaks the truth. We are partly to blame for the horrors that are taking place. Our tribes are killing each other."

Ivy nodded her head in agreement.

"I agree with Quake. We have failed our tribes," agreed Griffin, rubbing his chin in deep thought.

"Perhaps we have not succeeded in everything, but he still broke the law," Thekku spoke in obvious disagreement. "He formed a tribe whose loyalties are to each other and not to their own elemental kinds. Keepers are formed by six tribes and although we live in harmony together, we do not form bonds in the manner that these Light Bearers have done. They have also fought against their own kind and this means they have rejected the law of the keepers. It makes them no better than the rebel groups."

"So their greatest crime is not the bonds that were formed, but the unity that they've created?" asked Griffin incredulously. "Did the six of us not do exactly the same when the Ancient One chose us to lead?"

Ivy lifted an eyebrow as she looked at Thekku. Her voice sounded musical when she spoke. "Thekku, you are wrong my brother. We do form strong bonds between our tribes because we cannot survive without each other. Perhaps, if all the outpost groups were as fiercely loyal to each other as these Light Bearers have been, we would not be facing the threat of rebels. Will we not be forced to fight our own kind if these rebel groups attack us? The only grave wrong committed by Aire was that he did not consult us before forming his group of defenders."

"I say we vote then," said Tsunami furiously, his blue eyes icy cold. Snowflakes formed everywhere on his white clothes. "He and his team should be charged with treason."

"Then we shall vote," said Griffin. The black irises in his yellow eyes growing smaller into two perfect dark circles, giving him a fierce and dangerous appearance.

Quake stroked his goatee as he often did and asked, "Who votes that the Light Bearers are guilty of treason?"

Cyclone, Tsunami and Thekku raised their hands.

Quake asked again, "Who votes that the Light Bearers should not be charged with treason?" He lifted his own hand up in favour of the dismissal of the charge. Along with him, Griffin raised his hand. Everybody's eyes darted to Ivy, who sat in deep thought. They waited for a while and then Quake spoke again.

"Well, Ivy? What is your decision?"

She pouted her lips and looked directly at Aire. "Aire, although your intentions were honourable and brave, you still broke the law that says you are to respect and obey the elders of the tribes. You failed to ask permission before you formed a warrior group and in doing so, you also proved disloyal to the rulership. This confirms a charge of treason. So, I'm sorry, but I do find you guilty along with the rest of the Light Bearers. I believe they knew very well what their decision involved."

Shadow watched as the charge and ruling were written on the scroll and each elder placed a marking on it. Then they rolled the scroll up and sealed it with a symbol made from their respective elements. Cyclone sealed it with his breath, for air. Thekku placed a hardwood button on it and sealed the button with pressure, for wood.

Tsunami added rings of ice around it, for water. Ivy draped silver leaves around the circles of ice, for plants and Griffin rolled it into a soft wrap made of animal skin. Quake took the scroll and placed it into one of the holes in the wall of scrolls and then he sealed the hole with a red ruby stone, for earth. Hidden in the protective chamber of the rock wall, the scroll could only be retrieved with a representative from each tribe. Shadow heard Thekku demand that Aire be thrown in the underground cell again and that guards must be sent to arrest the remaining Light Bearers. Once they were all arrested, a suitable punishment for their crimes would be decided.

Yeah right, we'll see about that. The Light Bearers will not rot away in a prison. If these arrogant fools don't want our help, then we will do what we can for the sake of the tribes. If we must, we will leave Equilibria after we save it, Shadow thought. He was angry but knew that he had to control his emotions. He had to return to the Light Bearers, warn them, and together they needed to find a way to free Aire.

Chapter 20

Shadow looked into the bewildered eyes of his friends as he told them about the trial and the verdict. His brethren were especially upset that the elders had not seen reason and seemed less concerned that they were now considered traitors. After the disturbing news, they sat in silence.

"What now?" Muddy asked, pulling his hands through his hair, making it extra messy.

Raine lifted his eyebrow and looked at him as if he was foolish. "Are you daft? We go get Aire. We are not going to leave him to rot in a hole."

"Yes, I know, but what are we going to do after that? We've just become the hunted," Muddy replied solemnly.

Shadow laughed and sent a dagger playfully into a tree trunk. "The hunted, you say? Not if I can help it. Besides, the guards of the council are weak, even Lilly could take them out."

Lilly gave him a death stare but the smirk on his face did not fade.

"Fine, I get it. So, we are outlawed, but how do you plan to free Aire from the prison? That would be like walking into a dragon's lair," Muddy replied.

Dew stepped out from behind Raine. She smiled and her eyes lit up. "It doesn't have to be. I am from Par and I know the city well. It's a pity we don't have the map for the underground tunnels anymore, but I think I know my way above ground well enough."

Raine flashed his own pearly whites as he pulled the map from his pocket. Dew shook her head in disbelief. "But I thought you gave it to Aire?"

"I did, but when he made me second-in-command, he gave it to me. I suspect he had an idea that he might get locked up."

Maple's big brown eyes grew even bigger. She jumped down from the log she had been sitting on. "Oh, Aire! It is so like him to plan things in advance. I never thought I'd say it, but I miss him."

Shadow cleared his throat as he squatted on the ground. "Aire is not the only strategist around here; that's why he trained us. Let's have a look at our options."

Raine sat down next to Shadow, spreading the map open for all to see. Shadow twisted a twig between his fingers and motioned everyone closer. They discussed their possible entry points and the positions of everyone, but the task weighed heavily on them. The confusing maze of secret tunnels also did not help much.

Muddy dishevelled his hair again, as he snickered and announced, "I hope we don't get lost in these tunnels. That would end in a legendary failed rescue attempt."

The rest of the team looked at him in irritation.

"What?" he smiled looking silly.

"This is not a time for jokes, Muddy," Maple scolded him harshly.

He shrugged his shoulders. "Sorry, silliness keeps me sane."

Lilly spoke softly when she asked, "Just one question. How will we know where they keep Aire?"

"That's a good question," Shadow replied. "We will need to call on the help of Aire's friend, Skye. She will know where he is being kept."

"But how will we identify her?" Lilly asked.

Dew showed off her dimples again. "I know who she is."

Shadow shook his head. "No, we cannot risk being seen. I will ask the help of insects. They can deliver a message to Skye to meet us at the underground entry. It's the safest way."

Raine stood up. "Good. That settles it then. Fill your bellies my friends and get some rest. We leave when the moon is up."

The travel party left as planned but because they were journeying together, they did not make use of their individual special means of travelling. Raine was the first one to mutter a complaint when he saw Dew's flushed cheeks. They had walked a distance already and the aqualings were a little bit annoyed. They missed the stream with its fast currents.

"We are almost there," Muddy encouraged as he looked over his shoulder and saw that Lilly had a few scratches on her arms caused by the dry bushes that they had passed. The terrain was harsh – clear signs that the forest was dying.

Maple rolled her eyes. "You're all such younglings," she accused, sweeping her hand across her brow to remove some dust.

They had not travelled much further when they reached an area that was less dense. Shadow appeared out of nowhere.

"Wow! Stop," Muddy cried out in surprise, holding up his hand.

"It's just me," Shadow said quietly as he walked towards them.

"You should stop that creepy stuff Shadow. You nearly gave me sand lumps," the earthling whined.

"We are being followed," Shadow informed them flatly, his dark eyes blending with the colour of the night.

Lilly's eyes grew bigger but before she could say anything, Raine cut her off abruptly. "So, we are hunted," he said with a menacing smile as he waited for Shadow's summary. "Yup ... Four males – two woodlings and two earthlings."

Maple rubbed her hands together in excitement and pouted her lips perkily. "Well, let's take care of them and move on. No time to waste."

The gang looked at her with amusement. Raine shook his head and uttered a chuckle. "Geez Maple, you've become quite bloodthirsty," he said, entertained by the unusual female.

"No, not at all Raine, I just want to practise a bit more."

Laughter erupted and Shadow had to quiet them down.

"I agree with Maple. We are short on time. I think they followed us here from the outpost. They must have gone there to arrest us. Once they found out that we were not there, they probably tracked our movements and followed us through the forest."

"We should split up and travel by our normal methods," Dew suggested.

Raine shook his head in disagreement. "No, we have to fight them. If we split up, we will waste too much time and they might conquer some of us individually. If we stick together, they will not be able to do so. Let's just fight in formation and everything should be over in no time," he said confidently.

"Okay, then let's ambush the suckers!" Maple exclaimed.

Raine cocked an eyebrow at her. "Maple, if you keep this up you might frighten away all possible lifemates."

Maple jiggled her pointy ears and rested her hands on her hips. "Raine, just because you and Dew are mated does not mean everyone wants to be mated. In fact, I might just challenge that law," she informed him sarcastically.

Muddy's amber eyes sparkled with mischief as he whispered to Lilly, "Who would want to keep up with her drama?"

They both smothered their laughter when Maple narrowed her eyes in suspicion and zoomed in on them.

Shadow's dark eyes scanned the surrounding area. "An ambush is a good idea. They will not expect one. Use the elements to camouflage yourselves," he instructed.

They quickly hid themselves amongst their related elements and waited for their pursuers to arrive. They didn't wait long before the four guards stepped into the clearing.

"This is where it stops," growled an earthling.

"Where did they go?" asked another. An eerie silence followed and then the earth shook violently, cracks forming around them.

"It's a trap!" shouted one and they tried to run away. Within seconds, plant creepers raked over the forest floor and up the legs of the shaken guards. They tripped and fell. The green leaves of the creepers sprouted uncontrollably, weaving thick nets in the process. It was not long before the guards were trapped. They could barely move and found it impossible to reach their weapons. A fierce battle cry echoed in their ears and then they heard the approaching sound of running feet. Maple was first to reach them, ready to battle. She looked down regretfully at the trapped guards.

"Is that it?" she shouted, clearly irritated. She swirled around as the rest of the Light Bearers circled them. She looked accusingly at Muddy and Lilly.

"You two took over everything! There is nothing for the rest of us to do."

Muddy shrugged his shoulders in dismissal as he gave her a big smile. Lilly just stared down at the ground.

"Well done," Raine praised them.

"You congratulate them?" Maple said in disbelief. Before he could answer her, Shadow stepped forward and placed his hand on her shoulder to calm her down.

"Maple, it's for the best. We don't want to spill unnecessary blood. Besides, you will have more than enough exercise once we reach Par." She eyed him warily without saying a word.

"We best get moving," Dew announced, pointing up at the moon, which was now high in the night sky.

Raine nodded and was about to stroll away, when he paused and asked, "Shadow, what about them?" Shadow smiled deviously.

"I've got a little detour planned for them," he said as he mimicked the sound of an owl. Four owls came down from the trees and landed in front of Shadow. The animal protector thanked them and then pointed towards the guards. One by one, he cut open the nets and disposed of the guards' weapons. Then he stood back and allowed an owl to pick one up and disappear into the night. When they were all gone, he turned around and said. "Well, that was fun."

"Where did you send them," Raine inquired, looking pleased.

"North-east. It will take them a few more hours to return to Par," he grinned.

"Naughty, naughty, but I like it," Maple commented, waving a forefinger in Shadow's face.

"Okay keepers, time is not waiting for us," Dew urged them on again. They resumed the last stretch of their trip in a much lighter spirit, although Maple was still a little bit upset about her loss of exercise.

Chapter 21

The Light Bearers soon found themselves hiding behind a rock, eyeing the entrance to the underground tunnels. It was hidden beneath the tall grass at the foot of a tree trunk, just outside Par.

They waited for a few minutes and then Maple murmured, "Where is this Skye female?"

Muddy, who crouched next to her, shifted slightly to the right to whisper in her hear. "Relax, Maple. She'll be here any moment now."

Raine motioned for them to keep quiet but it didn't stop Maple from replying in an almost shrieking voice, "Oh yeah? And how would you know? I'm not even sure we should trust her. We don't know her."

Muddy tried to keep his voice low. "It doesn't matter. Aire trusts her and if he does, so should we."

Raine scowled at them wondering, for what seemed like the hundredth time, why Aire had entrusted him with the group. "Cut it out you two or would you like us to join Aire in prison?"

The sound of a nightingale drew their attention to the entrance again. They saw some movement in the grass and then heard the reply of an owl.

"That's our signal from Shadow. Move to the entrance. And do try to be quiet," Raine commanded in a sarcastic manner.

They moved quickly and fought their way through the tall grass. Once they entered the hole in the tree, Shadow joined them and directed them to a tunnel on their right. It was then that they noticed her. Skye, Aire's friend, was standing in front of the tunnel, holding a torch. She smiled at them nervously. Muddy elbowed Shadow in the ribs and mumbled under his breath.

"Hmm, seems like another female will soon join us. She's pretty. I bet you Aire lost his head to this one. Or is that his heart?"

Shadow chuckled quietly in response.

When they stood before her, Skye curtsied quickly.

Raine stepped forward and said, "Skye, I believe? It's a pleasure to meet you. I'm Raine. Thank you for helping us." He quickly introduced her to the rest of the team.

Skye nodded quietly. "I'm happy to meet you. Aire spoke much of you."

They all stood there for a moment in a completely awkward silence, before Skye gestured with her hand towards the dark tunnel. "Let's not waste time. Follow me."

Muddy elbowed Shadow again. "Weird, she's even as straight-forward and bossy as Aire, or maybe it's just an airling trait," he murmured as he studied her quietly.

Maple narrowed her eyes and looked at Skye. "You're familiar with the secret tunnels?"

Skye kept her eyes fixed on the dark tunnel as they moved forward. She did not glance at Maple when she replied, "I have an idea where we should go. I often played in these tunnels as a youngling."

Her reply drew the attention of Shadow and his deep voice echoed through the stuffy tunnel. "I thought only the elders knew about the secret tunnels in the network. How is it then that you are familiar with them?"

Shadow's question got most of them thinking. Eyes grew bigger and frowns appeared on their faces as suspicion grew amongst them. Was it a trap? Skye read their expressions and realised that they distrusted her. She lifted an eyebrow as she sarcastically answered. "You don't honestly believe I would lead you into a trap, do you?"

Raine cleared his throat nervously. "We don't know you, Skye."

"I know who she is," Dew announced with a smile.

Skye looked at her and recognition flashed across her face. She recalled the aqualing beauty from Par. She nodded in acknowledgment as their eyes met. The rest of them looked at Dew questioningly, but it was Skye who shocked them. "Very well, I will tell you the truth. I am the daughter of Cyclone."

Gasps went up from Maple and Lilly. The males looked like they had seen an evil forest nymph.

"You're the daughter of Cyclone? By all that is sacred, we will be killed," Muddy blurted out.

"Well, then he will have to kill me too," Skye said dryly. "Allow me to clarify, please."

Raine motioned for her to continue.

"As a youngling, I followed my father around everywhere … to get his attention, you see." She bit her lip shyly. "One day I ended up in the maze of tunnels. He was not aware that I followed him down here. I found myself returning often after that day and soon it became my secret hideout. It has been years since I've been down here, but hopefully I will still find my way."

The party followed her in silence through the next few tunnels, turning left and then right and then left again. Keepers had superb vision in the dark and entering dark underground tunnels did not affect them, but for one like Shadow, who thrived on his freedom, the narrow walls made his skin crawl. He hoped that they would move quickly through the stuffy tunnels. He didn't like feeling trapped and was grateful that Skye had brought a torch. Although they didn't really need it, the light somehow calmed him. It seemed like they walked for a long time, before Skye stopped.

"Oh oh," she said doubtfully.

"That doesn't sound good," Lilly commented.

Skye turned around and looked at them with big eyes. "I'm afraid I may be a little lost. I'm not sure if we should turn left or right at the fork ahead. I'm sorry. It's just been so long since I've been down here. I tried to explain that to Aire the last time I took him refreshments, but he insisted." Her voice nearly cracked as she uttered the words.

"Mmm, you took him refreshments?" Muddy asked playfully.

Skye looked at him uncertainly. She didn't understand why he made her serving Aire sound like an offence.

"Muddy! Focus on the situation at hand. What does her feeding Aire have to do with her being unsure which way to go," Raine scolded harshly.

Shadow laughed and Raine looked at him frowning.

"Did I miss something, or did you two drink sour honey bush tea at your last meal?"

Shadow lifted both hands up in defence. "No. Sorry. It's really nothing. You are right. Let us concentrate on the problem," he defended, mischief twinkling in his eyes.

Raine stared at them doubtfully and then he stepped forward to place his hand on Skye's arm. "Don't worry Skye. We've got a map, but without your help it would have taken us hours to get through this maze."

She looked at him in disbelief. "You've got a map? But …"

Shadow stepped forward and cut them off. "No time for explanations now. Later. Let's hurry, before the sun greets us good morning."

Raine took out the map and Skye studied it carefully, finding the next entrance quickly. They followed the tunnel to the right and shortly found themselves in front of a trap door.

"This is it. This door leads to the holding chambers. Aire is down there," Skye announced.

Shadow pulled out a dagger. "How many guards?"

"Only one, but I doubt that you will need that," Skye answered, pointing to his dagger as she smothered the torch with a swift movement of her hand over the flame. Shadow frowned at her and then slipped the dagger back into his belt as he opened the door. They followed him slowly down the narrow passage.

Muddy looked at Skye with envy and whispered, "For a moment there I couldn't figure out how you killed that flame, but then I remembered that airlings can remove the air which fire needs to burn. It's a very cool trick."

Skye smiled back at him with big intelligent eyes. Somehow, her reaction made Muddy even more envious.

Shadow stopped and held up his hand, indicating with his head that the guard was just up ahead. He took out a blowpipe and filled it with a small wooden dart. After aiming, he blew. The dart flew through the air and struck the neck of the guard. Grabbing at his neck, the guard turned around speedily and stared at Shadow with a dazed look in his eyes. Then he fell down like a rock.

"Did you kill him?" Lilly asked nervously.

Shadow smiled sneakily.

"No, he is just asleep. The point of the dart is coated with a sleep mixture. He will wake up after a while, with a terrible headache," he commented, packing his blowpipe away.

They found Aire sitting up on his straw pallet, smiling at them. "Greetings! Brethren, what took you so long?" He jumped to his feet in one fluid movement to greet them. Maple flew into Aire's arms.

"Brute, I thought I would never hear your scolding again," she pestered.

The males greeted him in the way of the warriors, grabbing each other's forearms, while the females gave him hugs.

When Aire hugged Skye and thanked her, Muddy frowned and joked, "Holding on a little tight there, my friend?" Everyone laughed as Aire gave him an irritated glance.

"Why, are you jealous, Muddy? " Raine teased.

"I don't think he missed me that much," Aire mumbled in male defence.

"Oh, no you are wrong, Aire. I did," Muddy said.

Aire quirked an eyebrow at him and pulled his hand through his hair. "You did?"

"Oh yes. Well actually, we all did. Raine here is a real bully when he is in charge," Muddy complained, pulling a face at Raine.

Raine chuckled and added, "Muddy, you complain worse than a female."

"What did you just say?" Maple raised her voice, scorn dripping from her lips.

"Oops," Muddy mocked as he looked at Raine, his amber eyes shining like gems. Raine's face grew red as Dew moved in front of him and gave him a stare of death. Aire shook his head and a playful spark lit up his eyes. He added insult to injury as he slapped Raine playfully on the shoulder and said, "Well, well. It seems to me that the females took charge of the Light Bearers in my absence."

They broke out in laughter and enjoyed their reunion. Shadow disappeared behind the door again and returned with the slumped body of the guard. He dragged the guard into the chamber and rested him neatly on Aire's pallet.

"He needs the rest," he mumbled and tugged his two thumbs into his trousers' waistband, as he slumped against the chamber wall, kicking one foot back to steady himself against it. Then he flashed them pearly white teeth. Aire studied his dark warrior and a glint of appreciation passed in his eyes as he slowly dipped his head. Maple noticed and rolled her eyes in response.

"Shadow, be careful not to grow fat with pride. Argon might then refuse to allow you on his back," she teased.

Their moment of happiness was short-lived, as the earth suddenly shook and thunder cracked in the sky. Next they heard screaming and a guard shouting, "Attack! The city is under attack!"

The Light Bearers looked around in panic.

"No! We are too late. The city is under attack," Maple cried.

Aire moved quickly and gestured them towards the prison door. "We need to get out of here and devise a plan of action," he roared.

"Follow me," Skye replied coolly and they all ran for the trapdoor which lead back into the underground tunnels.

"Tread carefully, we cannot afford for these tunnels to cave in on us," Shadow said.

Muddy looked annoyed. "Did you forget I am one of the few earthlings who can move the ground with nothing but my words?"

Shadow placed another careful step and responded, "No offence Muddy, but I still don't think I would like to get buried underground. Not even if it is for a short while. I don't like to feel trapped."

Skye whispered, "In here," as she opened another trapdoor that lead into living chambers.

"Where are we?" Lilly asked.

"Welcome to my home. This is a hidden chamber beneath my dwelling. We can hide here for a while before we go above ground," she answered, clamping her hands together behind her back, the look in her eyes reflecting the serene sound of her voice.

Aire rubbed his chin and smiled at her. "Interesting … Skye, you are very resourceful."

Muddy flashed another silly grin as he looked at Aire and then back at Skye. He repeated the action again but stopped abruptly when Aire's eyes bored into him, flashing an unspoken warning. Muddy swallowed the lump in his throat and moved towards a seat. *Who would have thought that serious Aire could become even more serious? Obviously, this lifemate business has a weird effect on the males,* he decided and his now averted eyes stared intently at a spot on the floor of the chamber. He could still sense Aire watching him and he felt like a youngling who had just been scolded.

Chapter 22

The sound of a horn echoed through the night and Aire closed his eyes, even as all the others darted theirs to his. His expression was pained.

"It's the signal for danger, announcing the call to retreat to the palace. The city is under attack. They will soon close the gate to prevent the rebels from entering," he told them.

Raine pulled Dew closer to him and held her tight in a plea of forgiveness for his previous uncaring words. He hoped she would see it as a gesture of him offering her protection. The time had finally arrived; Par was under attack and the thought of losing his newfound love was unbearable. Yet, they were called to be warriors and they would soon face the inevitable. He pressed his nose into her hair and inhaled the fresh scent of clean water before he spoke.

"Yes, once everyone is inside, it will keep the rebels out of the palace. The keepers should remain safe in there … for now at least," he said, straightening his shoulders as if to gather his last bit of confidence for what was to come.

Lilly bit her lip anxiously and her long lashes blinked rapidly. "What do we do now?"

Aire looked at her sympathetically. "We fight, Lilly," he said wearily. "As much as I wished this moment would never arrive, unfortunately it has. We tried our best to prevent it, but the elders' rejection of our path has left us with nothing but each other. I said before that if they rejected our path, we would need to make a choice between our loyalty to them or the survival of our race. That time has come. I will understand if you choose not to fight. I cannot guarantee anything," he said with great sorrow, rubbing both hands over his face.

"But how? Surely we are outnumbered," she reasoned.

Aire expelled his breath with a sigh. "We have an advantage. Even as we speak, the rest of the keepers are scrambling to the main keep. Once there, they will hold the gate and prevent the rebels from entering. If some of the rebels do manage to enter – the commanders, tribe elders and guards will defend the palace. Outside only a few guards will remain to fight. We will join them and do what we are trained to do. We fight as one. Whatever enemy is above ground will not be able to withstand our force."

Lilly still looked puzzled and he dropped to his knees, taking a twig and drawing the schematic representation of his words. When he saw that she understood, he shifted his weight and crouched, resting on his hind legs.

Aire looked at the team of warriors seated around him on the chamber floor and on what little seats were available in Skye's humble chamber.

"Are you prepared to die for the existence of our race?" he asked them bluntly as he rubbed the twig between his forefinger and thumb, as if its rotation could somehow break the nervous spell that had fallen over him. There was no more time for honourable beliefs. Now was the time to stand by those ideals and he hoped that they realised this.

Shadow cracked his knuckles. "What's the difference? If we don't die today, we will die soon enough. The forest is fading and without the united body to care for it, every keeper in Equilibria will also die. I say we fight and stand a chance to save some keepers who, in return, can continue our way of life."

Raine cleared his throat. "As much as I don't like the idea of dying, I agree with Shadow. It's better to try and create a chance than to do nothing and perish."

"I took my pledge and I may not always be serious, but my word is honourable," Muddy added. Aire's eyes found his and he nodded, quietly agreeing with his sentiment and then his eyes sought out the females.

"What about you?" he asked.

Maple nearly jumped up to answer him. "I will fight."

Dew nodded in promise and so did Lilly. Aire looked at Skye with sparkling eyes. Strange how the silver-haired female could make him feel pleased even in the midst of terrible circumstances.

"You are under no obligation to fight with us, Skye."

A small smile formed on her lips. "I know Aire, but I want to be part of this cause. I fight."

Aire released a breath he was not even aware of holding, as relief flooded through him. It seemed like his bunch of crazies were honourable to the core. It pleased him immensely. Narrow-eyed, Shadow raised his head and took out a dagger to inspect it, running it slowly over the palm of his hand. "Chief, there is one more thing."

"Yes, Shadow what is it?"

"The forest is dying and we are about to go out there and fight those who are responsible for maintaining it. Not everyone will perish in this battle, but the ones left will never be able to bounce back and fulfill all the duties. We need some kind of intervention," he said.

Maple glanced at Shadow and wondered how he managed to stay confident under the most dangerous of circumstances.

Aire rubbed his chin as his gaze moved around the chamber. "You are right. The same thought has been plaguing me. The only idea I have is that one of us should go to the top of Mount Dashar and summon the Ancient One. He should be informed that the forest is dying and so also our race. I don't know much about him, but from what I've heard, he might be our last hope – if it is true that he formed the tribes." He murmured the last part, not comfortable enough to acknowledge to his friends that he had his doubts. Silence met his announcement. No one liked it. Aire shifted and his expression darkened.

"Fellow Light Bearers, hear me now. We must do what we must to preserve our way of life. It will not be easy, but this is not just about us, it is for the greater good of Equilibria and its inhabitants."

"Who shall go? We are only eight and we all need to fight," Lilly added with anxiety in her voice. Shadow popped the dagger back into his belt.

"I will," he said dryly.

Maple quickly replied, "No, you cannot. We need you in the battle. I will ask the trees to assist us."

Everybody looked at her in surprise.

"Exactly how do you plan to do that, Maple?" Muddy exclaimed, glancing at Aire for assistance, at the same time trying to hide his amusement.

Obviously Maple did not think this through. How on earth are the trees going to deliver a message? Animals perhaps, but not trees … and they call me the comical one, he thought.

Aire looked at her thoughtfully. "Well?" he prompted. "Tell us exactly how you intend to do this, Maple. I've never heard of trees delivering messages."

Maple rolled her eyes and sighed. "I am a woodling, you know. I can call on the help of the trees, just like any of you can call on the help of your elements. The trees are ancient and they have always been able to communicate. Not in the same manner as we do, but they give warning scents of danger."

"How?" Muddy asked suspiciously, arching an eyebrow.

"Through the scents and oils that they excrete, duh huh," she muttered.

Aire rubbed his chin again. "Calm down now. Surely Maple knows what she's talking about. We need to trust her abilities. It sounds like a plan to me."

Muddy still wanted to argue, but Aire did not want to hear any of it. The earthling was convinced that the trees would not be able to deliver the message … a very important message at that. Eventually they agreed that Maple would ask the trees and that Shadow would ask Argon to do the same. Skye cleared her throat and pulled a stray strand of hair behind her pointy ear.

"At least we know that the rebels cannot enter the palace through any of the secret tunnels because we have the map. I will lead you to a tunnel that will get us just outside the city. From there, Shadow and Maple can send their messages. It will also give us time to survey the area and plan our attack," she said thoughtfully.

"Well then, let's not waste any more time. We've got a city to hold and a battle to win. Let's get moving," Aire ordered.

Muddy whispered in Shadow's ear. "I told you he likes her. He even follows suit." They both chuckled softly and followed the rest of the group into the tunnels again. Once outside the city, Shadow called Argon by mimicking the squawk of a raven. Soon the impressive bird of prey landed next to him. He pattered the bird gently and whispered words of praise to him. Argon lowered his head and rubbed his beak slowly against Shadow's hand. The rest of the team stared in amazement at the strange relationship between the protector and his fierce bird. It was the only time that Shadow ever appeared vulnerable. And the only time that his fierce bird seemed almost approachable. Their eyes held for a few seconds, everyone intently aware of their wordless communication as Shadow imparted his instruction telepathically. Argon blinked his topaz eyes a few times and then he took off in flight, crying *keewoowee* in a most piercing way.

Maple walked over to one of the older trees and laid her head and her hands on it. She took her time to speak softly to the old tree, gently rubbing its bark.

Then she turned around and smiled at the others as she walked towards them. "It's done," she said as she passed Muddy.

Muddy stared at her doubtfully and then shrugged his shoulders in dismissal. Moments later the intoxicating scent of pine and sweet forest invaded his senses. *Perhaps the trees can communicate after all*, he thought, a smile on his lips. It was strange that they had known each other for so long, yet only now in the face of adversity, was what was hidden in their hearts revealed.

The eight of them hid behind a rock as they glanced at the battlefield. It was horrendous. There was blood everywhere. Keepers were engaged in heavy combat with each other, using blades, axes and hammers. Raine shook his head in despair. "So, the earthlings and airlings attack first. The guards are weak, outnumbered and incapable of holding up. We'd better get out there."

Aire nodded in agreement and then his gaze moved around to everyone. "I see the airlings attack under the leadership of Windy. Don't let his charm and good looks fool you. Sly at times, he might fight without honour if he wills to do so. He loves nothing more than to win and will do anything to obtain victory. Look out for tricks from the airlings. They will try to blow dust into your eyes and spin you into whirlwinds," he warned them.

Muddy saw Soil cutting the throat of a guard and suddenly Aire's voice sounded far away. He saw and heard nothing anymore, his eyes big with fear.

He took a deep breath; held it for a minute and then exhaled slowly, shaking his head. "I am so dead if Soil gets his filthy hands on me. He promised that he would give me a slow and painful death if I lied, and ... I lied," he said softly, concern straining his voice.

Shadow slapped him gently on the shoulder. "Relax my brother. I've got you covered. You will die, but not today," he assured, a devious smile on his lips. "That bully will not lay a hand on you. Besides, I need some practise and I reckon he will make a fine target."

Muddy smiled nervously. "Thanks. That gives me a measure of comfort."

Aire dragged a hand through his hair. "Light Bearers, remember we must act as one. Our enemy cannot fight using the combined force of the elements, so they will mainly use weapons. You may use weapons but our main tactic remains the combination of our elemental functions. Maple, Shadow and Lilly, you must work together. Lilly weave traps on the forest floor to ambush the earthlings. Maple, use the tree branches to ensnare the airlings and then push them into Lilly's traps. Shadow, use your arrows to keep them in those traps and protect us wherever you can. The rest of us will form whirlwinds, mudslides and thunderstorms. Look out for the opportunity and communicate with each other when to join the elements. Anything we can do together will work to our advantage."

Everyone nodded in agreement.

Aire stood up, paused and then he swung around again. His darkened eyes scanned over them. "One last thing, should anyone fall today, you should know that it will be as heroes and not as criminals. It breaks my heart that the elders failed to see our role in all of this but, when I look at you, I know that you have become the light of Equilibria. Our race … the keepers of Equilibria … depends on us. Stand firm, stand together and remember our purpose."

They all grabbed each other's hands and cried, "For light and honour," before storming onto the battlefield, moving as a well-orchestrated unit.

Aire and Skye's forms became see-through and bolts of electricity charged all around them. Raine and Dew became as shiny as the surface of a lake and the light that reflected from them blinded everyone. Muddy's vibrant bronzed skin, mixed with the deep copper colour of his hair, resembled mighty flames of gold. Shadow the warrior of formidable stealth; his aura darkened even more and intimidated those around him. Lilly's cloak of purple, silver and jade flashed like a precious gem and Maple looked like an accomplished heroine, while the intricate designs of the golden bands on her forearms shone brightly. The transformation of the Light Bearers into their warrior forms was a sight to behold. Honour drove them forward into battle.

Chapter 23

oforic and the young males continued to walk until the scent of lavender filled their nostrils. They were still walking along slippery slopes, but the peaks were growing lusher with green moss spread all over. Cliffs still surrounded them, but beneath the slope lay the remote, almost hidden, green haven. Sheltered by the great Mount Dashar, the stronghold of the keepers was carpeted with green grass, purple lavender fields and big old trees. The creeks looked like silver veins, glistening in the sun. Boforic cleared his throat.

"Finally lads, we've made it. Ah … Par, still as lovely as ever," he sighed. "We still have time, so we can rest for a moment and then move down into the valley." His eyes filled with admiration for the beautiful scene below them.

They found a few rocks under a small tree and sat down comfortably. Soon the dwarf rubbed his big belly and dug into his bag. He found a few figs and berries.

"Tis the last of our food, so it's a good thing we're nearly there," he mumbled, as he divided the food amongst them. They nibbled on the treats and took a few sips of water from a leaf which Drizzle filled. Giggling excitedly, Boforic grasped the small hands of the three young males.

"I should thank ye lads. I know ye could have travelled much faster, but ye saw it fit to accompany a slow dwarf. Well, now don't say that I didn't thank ye. Aye, twas a pleasure to travel with ye."

Airon smiled cheerfully as he asked, "We met you very far in the southern part of the forest. Where did you come from Boforic?"

The dwarf rubbed his nose thoughtfully. "We dwarves come from the big, icy mountains in the north, but aye, I did visit in the far south. I had me some business to attend to there. Signing of treaties, much like it was done here in Par, years ago."

"Ah ha! Which brings us back to the legend," exclaimed Dusty, pulling his mohawk in a more upright position.

Boforic frowned and shook his head. "Lads, in case ye did nay notice, we're going to be down there in the next hour," he said, as he pointed down into the valley. Everybody burst out laughing as the shy Drizzle nearly fell off his rock to object.

"Nay!" he shouted.

"But ye can hear the end once we attend the great council. The elders will tell ye everything again," Boforic replied with a frown.

"They will not tell us everything the way you do. Please, finish the tale," the aqualing pleaded with sorrowful eyes. Boforic couldn't resist the young male's sincerity and pulled in a deep breath, before he expelled it with a slow sigh.

"Okay, aye. I will continue the tale until we reach Par."

"Yes!" cried Drizzle and he jumped up to hug one of Boforic's legs. His two friends stared at him in disbelief. Drizzle was normally timid. Boforic was completely uncomfortable and did not know how to react, but then found himself patting the young keeper's head awkwardly.

They rested in the shade for a little while longer and then descended into the valley, following the small footpaths and moving with care. Boforic coughed, cleared his throat and resumed the tale.

Shadow's dark brows furrowed above his eyes as he scanned the battlefield. The stench of blood burned in his nostrils as keepers fought each other. Soil spotted Muddy and was rapidly closing in on him. Soil let out a groan and lifted a blade above his head with the intention to drive it through the red-head's body.

Shadow whispered, "Oh no, you don't," as he aimed and pulled at his bowstring.

His arrow struck Soil in the shoulder, the force taking him down instantly. Muddy swung around and looked his enemy in the face.

"It was supposed to be slow and painful, Soil," he said with a grin, as he kicked the earthling into one of the traps. As soon as he landed on the leaf stem net, it jerked him up high and then sprang back just short before it hit the ground. Soil barked out a few threats and tried to escape, but to no avail. He was trapped in the net, dangling from a branch.

Muddy shouted, "Thanks!" as he ran to assist Maple and Lilly, who were engaged in combat with two airlings.

Fighting back-to-back, Maple and Lilly stood their ground. Maple ground her teeth and swung two blades at her rival. He stormed at her, but hesitated when he saw the two blades.

"You think you're brave, woodling?" he said in a grim voice. She lifted an eyebrow.

"No, I am lethal, airy one. By the way, the grim voice does not suit your pretty face," she answered with a sneaky smile and charged forward again.

An arrow whizzed past her and her foe fell to the ground with the arrow protruding from his thigh.

Maple threw her hands up in the air as she shouted, "Now look what you've done, Shadow! You took away all my fun!"

Lilly swept the hair away from her eyes as she cried out. "Watch your step Maple; you nearly slit my throat with that blade."

Maple rolled her eyes as she ran towards another opponent, the sound of clashing steel followed. Muddy teamed up with Lilly and the two of them moved together, deflecting and delivering blows as though part of a rehearsed dance.

Aire whirled around and deflected another mighty blow. He twisted up again and collided with another airling in the process. They both came down hard to the ground. The airling moved quickly, pinned him down and then just as he was about to drag his blade over Aire's throat, an arrow slammed into his back. The foe sank to his knees and then his limp body fell on Aire's chest. Aire's eyes followed the path from where the arrow had come and his eyes met the dark raven eyes of Shadow. His friend winked at him and then swooshed around to dispatch another arrow.

Aire barely had time to breathe, when a deafening cry pierced his thoughts. It was Skye. His gaze sought her out amongst the chaos and he saw her swinging a blade downwards and then stabbing her rival in the thigh. Then she swung around again and deflected another blow. *Wow! She's potent,* he thought and pride swelled in his chest. Just then, another rival stormed him with a huge axe. The earthling was big and his once beautiful sparkling ruby eyes were now shadowed with menace. Aire continued to attack and defend himself, when Raine suddenly cut a straight path past him, to the spot where Dew was fighting.

Dew's arms were growing weary and she had difficulty lifting the blade. Her rival was an earthling and he acted like a cat toying with his food. Raine charged forward and closed his hand over Dew's. He clutched the blade and then lifting it over her shoulder, brought it down with a crushing swipe, severing the arm of the foe. He quickly pressed his lips to the back of her head and spun around again to deflect an axe coming down on them. Moments later, their rival was defeated when Raine delivered blow after blow to his stomach.

He heard Aire shout, "Storm," and then they joined him and Skye to form a formation. Soon they twirled together, lightning bolts and rain filling the sky. Many rivals got trapped in the whirlwinds, which threw them down hard, leaving them unconscious. Muddy teamed up with Raine and the two of them worked up a mud pool. Soon the heavy rainfall caused the upper levels of the ground to become unstable. The resulting quick-moving mudslide took out a number of foes, leaving them worn-out.

Aire looked around and saw that the battle site was a dreadful mess. Most of the enemy was defeated through the natural weapons used, but a bunch of them grouped at the gate of the palace, trying to break through.

"To the palace gate," his voice thundered as he charged, jumping up high, with his blade above his head. Just then, he heard waves crashing and the unmistakable smell of grass and oak filled the air.

"Oh, no!" he heard himself say, as he turned around and saw the armies of aqualings, zoionlings, woodlings and plantlings approaching. They were joining the battle. Shadow's deep voice shook him out of his shocked state. "So, it's a war after all."

The Light Bearers stood together, facing their opponents in dismay. The remaining earthlings and airlings charged forward to meet their adversaries on the battlefield. Aire shook his head. He wasn't sure what to say or what their next move should be. Now that the rebels of the other tribes had joined, the destruction of Par could be rapid.

A group of aqualings forced the palace gate open with a destructive gush of water. Soon more guards and common keepers spilled onto the battlefield and engaged in the battle. It was a painful sight as the damaging forces of the natural elements destroyed the lower valley. Lightning split trees, areas were flooded and the earth shook in anger. The rebels fought not only against each other but also against the peaceful residents of Par. Animals were crying out in pain and the peace left the forest as chaos descended upon Par. The once beautiful city now resembled nothing but ruins.

The Light Bearers tried to stop as many blows as possible. In their hearts, they were not sure if any keeper could survive, but they fought bravely and united as one force, honouring their covenant with one another.

Chapter 24

The party of four entered the tranquil Par and curious faces peeked at them from everywhere. "I suppose they're all looking at me," Boforic mumbled self-consciously. Airon broke out in laughter, Dusty and Drizzle following shortly. They found it most amusing that Boforic was not comfortable under the scrutinising stares of their kind. It also reminded them how they reacted the first time they had seen the dwarf.

"Shall we make our way to the great hall then, lads?" Boforic asked curiously.

The three young males exchanged glances and all together came to a halt. Boforic kept moving, but soon realised that his companions were not following him. He turned around slowly and let out a sigh, his shoulders slumping. "Now lads, ye canna be serious. The council will be held soon. We still have time to fill our bellies and mine is rumbly as it is. The tribe elders and the older keepers will tell ye the tale again and then ye will find out about the ending."

The males scowled and did not move. Nor did any of them utter a word. It amused the dwarf that even the happy-go-lucky Airon showed a serious side.

He shook his head and grimaced. "Och lads, I am too old for ye games. I said until we reach the city. Look around ye, we are here now," he said, waving his arms to point at their surroundings. Silence followed and puzzled faces glared up at him.

"Are ye playing dumb?" They just stared at him. Boforic went a little bit red in his face. Finally, he threw both hands up in the air.

"Och, okay. I will finish the tale, but only if I can calm me rumbly tummy," he added, rubbing his stomach. The three young males launched themselves at him and hugged whatever part of him they could reach. Two hung onto his legs and another grabbed his hand. The old dwarf let out a rumble of laughter and they proceeded towards the main keep.

Inside the great hall, a lovely plantling named Rose served them delicious cuisine on trenchers and skins of honey bush tea to fill their goblets. Boforic smiled as he noticed that the hall was neat and tidy, but not as fancy as it used to be. While they waited for the hour of the council meeting, the young males did not touch any of the food, but were enthralled with the tale. The dwarf on the other hand, swiped his knuckles over his mouth and continued to stuff himself as he told them the last part of the legend.

Devastation and despair increased in the midst of metal upon metal, loud cries and forces of nature out of control. It was in the moment of their worst darkness that Aire suddenly saw the battlefield light up significantly. Glorious light descended upon them. When he looked up, he saw a light as bright as the sun drawing near from the slope of Mount Dashar. It blinded him and he had to shield his eyes from it. The sound of thunder, rain, wind and crashing waves filled the air, but none of these forces were visible … only the blinding light. It came to a standstill in the valley, close to the big Oak. Keepers of every size and tribe drew near to witness the strange phenomenon. The tribe elders moved forward and fell down on their knees.

"Ancient One! We acknowledge your presence," cried Cyclone. The crowd stood in absolute awe. The Ancient One was right there in their midst. They couldn't see much except for the light, but could make out a figure similar to their own in the glow of it. Then he spoke and the forest went silent in the absence of the usual wind and chirping of birds. Without any of the familiar sounds, their surroundings suddenly became eerie. *Which one of you summoned me,* he asked with a voice like music. The keepers were shocked when Aire and the rest of the Light Bearers moved through the crowd and came to a standstill in front of the Ancient One, as close as his bright light allowed them to.

The Light Bearers bowed slowly. Aire cleared his throat anxiously, the mark on his wrist shining ever so brightly. "Ancient One … we are the ones who called you. We thank you for coming. I believe it is obvious why we summoned you. Our race has reached the point of destruction. We didn't know what else to do."

Some of the rebels grunted, but quickly swallowed their murmurs when the Ancient One lifted an arm and said, *Silence.*

Aire continued nervously to present his case and he told the Ancient One about all that had happened. Time stood still as they all waited for him to speak again. Then the music flowed.

"Equilibria literally means perfect balance. Everything in this forest existed in perfect balance, even you did. Look around you, keepers of Equilibria. You have destroyed everything that was entrusted to you. I created you to form part of this whole, so that you may co-exist and take care of the balance. Yet, you have allowed evil to consume you, and everything else around you.

Earthlings look at the ground. It calls to me in mourning. I have formed you from the earth; you are one and the same. I gave you the ability to guide and work with the earth and all its aspects so that you might live and be honoured through it. In the same way that you supply to the earth, it supplies to you.

Out of shame, not a single earthling was able to lift a head. Every last one of them could feel the words cut at their hearts.

Airlings, you I formed from the air. Your substances are one and the same, honed together with purpose and harmony. Now the air reeks of the stench of rotting carcasses. Their blood is on your hands.

Loud gasps went up from the airlings as the truth of his words hit them.

Aqualings, the colour of the water has changed. What was once healthy and clear has now become cloudy and sorrowful, just like your own hearts. You have defiled yourselves.

Every other keeper sensed the heaviness of the sorrow that penetrated the aqualings as the words sunk deep into their hearts.

"Ancient One, we have tried to tell them so," Cyclone interrupted.

Did you, Cyclone? All the elders that I have chosen to rule over this race are clothed in finery, but their hearts have become as dead as the forest.

More gasps went up from the crowd of keepers.

Why are you all so surprised? You pretend that everything is fine, yet Equilibria is dying at your hands and your race is destroying itself. Is this what I have commanded you to do?

A few heads shook and some bowed in shame.

I should destroy all of you.

"No, please don't. We plantlings have not neglected our duties," Ivy pleaded.

No, Ivy, you have. I formed you from the greenery of the forest and the same sap that flows in the veins of plants, is mixed with your blood and flows in your veins too. Your life force is bound to plants.

Woodlings, you were made in the same manner. The uprightness of the plants and trees are also yours, yet, they too are dying as we speak. Soon you might join them.

The faces of the green plantlings turned white and the woodlings bark clothing cracked with fear. His sorrowful tune continued as he looked to the zoionlings.

Zoionlings, you are called zoionlings because you are formed from and for the animals. You were supposed to protect them, yet they too are losing their breath."

Then Griffin raised his hand. "Ancient One, we have not killed the forest. It was the other tribes."

You have all killed the forest. If you injure one toe on your foot, does your entire body not suffer? The complete body experiences the pain. You were created to function as one system; therefore, no tribe can survive without the others. If one tribe dies, all the tribes will die. Just like the plants need the earth and water to grow in, the animals need the plants to live. They both need air to breathe and so too is it with the tribes. You are all intertwined and no tribe can stand alone and survive. You have not just harmed the forest; you have harmed your livelihood and yourselves. You are all different, yet the same, because you all form part of one body. Can you not see that it is in working together that those very differences give you strength? You don't just belong to the forest and each other, but also to me ... the one who made you. You are a body that reflects my work.

The music stopped and the keepers looked at each other and their surroundings.

"What have we done?" cried some, and many wept in shame. Others hugged and pleaded for forgiveness. The Ancient One watched them as they showed remorse.

What shall it be keepers? Will you continue on your course of destruction or are you willing to make amends?

They all wanted things to go back to the way it was. Once they realised that they all might die, power and greed did not appeal anymore.

Good, then let's get on with restoration and peace. First, you will all promise never to fight another keeper again and to always respect the other tribes. You will also pledge your service to the forest and all that lives within it. You must sign a treaty that will bind you to your promise in honour, much like the honourable Light Bearers did.

"The Light Bearers?" exclaimed Thekku. "What is so honourable about them? They dishonoured our laws."

The Ancient One paced up and down in front of the keepers and his glow followed him.

They were the only ones who upheld the most important law of the keepers. They stood together in adversity and refused to split. The rest of you satisfied your selfish desires and turned against each other. You allowed evils such as pride, greed and jealousy to rule over you. They fought for the survival of your race, while you, the tribe elders, turned a blind eye to the problems. You got too comfortable with your status and fineries. They are the true heroes of Equilibria and they have my respect.

The crowd was at first quiet, but then Griffin clapped his hands and cheered the Light Bearers. The rest of the crowd soon followed his example. Some of the strongest males lifted them up on their shoulders and they were exalted amongst the tribes. The moment was magnificent as all the tribes showed them honour.

Laughter erupted from a nearby bush and a funny looking male with long hair and beard appeared before them. Recognition dawned as they realised it was their previous guest, Boforic. They grew silent as they stared at him, every single keeper wondering what he was doing there. He lifted his thick eyebrows and skipped in circles as he came closer to them and then he bowed low before the Ancient One.

"Greetings! Ancient One. Aye, I came as soon as I could."

The Ancient One greeted him and introduced him formally as not only a dwarf from the mountains, but also as an ancient law keeper.

Boforic is here to sign the treaty as a witness. Every two decades, he will come and read the law to your race again. When he is no more, another member of his race will continue in his stead. This must be done to remind you and every young keeper of your purpose. You must teach your young and in so doing, safeguard the survival of your race.

The keepers agreed to this and although they were skeptical at first, they soon warmed up to the idea that the funny looking dwarf from the mountains would become a regular guest of Equilibria. Boforic walked forward and stood on the far left side of the Ancient One. The Ancient One kept quiet and watched them from a distance. He had the power to destroy them but he wanted to give them another chance, because he treasured the forest with its little keepers.

Boforic pulled out a scroll and read from it.

"Keepers of Equilibria, you are an ancient, noble race. For thousands of years your kind has taken care of this beautiful forest. Although the responsibility of this task is not an easy one, the plants and animals rely on your ability to influence the natural elements and sustain their livelihood. Nature can take care of itself, but if Equilibria was left to its fate, it would lose its enchanting beauty and mysticism. It might even die, like many other forests already have. In his wisdom, the Ancient One created you, a special race, to ensure the survival of this forest. You have now learned first-hand that your destiny is bound to this forest and each other. If the forest dies, you too will not survive. You must work together as one to ensure its survival. You must vow today to serve the forest and all that lives in it, as one body, to honour all tribes and not to allow evil to bring separation between you again. Will you do this?"

The tribe elders came forward and every team commander from the outposts joined them. They all took the vows as the dwarf read them out to each tribe individually. That day the tribes signed the treaty on another scroll and the dwarf was witness to their promise. Boforic placed his own signature on the scroll and vowed to bring judgment upon the race, should they fail to uphold their pledge.

Soon afterwards, they had a feast to celebrate the restoration of their kind and the peace that ruled over them. There was no need to bury the dead; their essence returned to the elements that they were made from. And although lives were lost, the greater event of peace overshadowed it and that was cause enough for celebration. Boforic joined the elders and had them laughing and playing silly games with him in no time. The law keeper was not just stoic; he had a comical side to him too.

After receiving many gestures and words of honour from others, the Light Bearers finally sat together quietly and shared a meal. There were no adequate words to describe their emotions. After some time, Shadow stretched out his left arm and held up his wrist for all to see. His mark was glowing brightly. He smiled, "It is a privilege to be a keeper of the forest, but an honour to be a Light Bearer." More smiles erupted from the group of eight and a few eyes grew watery. Raine looked into the eyes of his mate and then he looked at her wrist. His eyes widened in the realisation that she did not bear the mark.

"I think we forgot that two more Light Bearers still need to make their pledge," he said, his gaze resting on Dew.

Aire smiled as he looked at Skye.

"They don't need a mark to say that they are Light Bearers; they've proved their worth through their actions. However, I would gladly bestow the mark upon Dew, the mate of my friend Raine."

Then he took Skye's hand and raised an eyebrow. "As the mate of Aire, son of Atmos and the commander of the Light Bearers, I would also gladly bestow the mark upon Skye."

Maple gasped in shock. "Did you ask Skye to be your mate?"

Aire smiled broadly and touched Skye's face gently as he spoke. "I'm asking her now. Skye, will you honour me and be my mate?"

Skye's eyes grew bigger and she flung herself into Aire's arms. "Yes! I will," she answered.

He kissed her and sealed their fate.

Muddy, sitting next to Shadow, threw his hands up in the air. "I knew it!" he cried out. "It seems like I have a gift to sense these things. Shadow, my dark friend, I suspect your brooding days are also numbered," he joked, wiggling his eyebrows at Shadow.

Shadow shook his head and chuckled at the remark. "Muddy, my brave friend, we can wager that you stand next in line," he countered with an easy smile.

For a moment, Muddy looked panic-stricken, but soon enough he hid his unease behind a mask of carelessness. After all, as much as he doubted that he would mate, the prospect of Shadow mating was less. They all shared some more laughter and then Aire led the new members into their pledge and gave them their markings.

The keepers continued their celebrations until dawn. They made music, danced and shared in the joy of each other. The Ancient One took one last look at the jolly crowd and then his light grew smaller as he ascended to the top of the mountain, not to be seen again for a long time. Not far away a piercing *keewoowee* sound echoed in the sky and Shadow responded with the squawk of a raven, to bid his companion a good rest. Soon he too would have to retreat and work through his mixed emotions.

Despite the glory of the Light Bearers and the joy of restoration, the heart of the stealth warrior was heavy. He had lost his brother Hunter in the battle, yet he told himself that his loss was nothing compared to that which the rest of the keepers and Raven were experiencing. Raven … the beautiful little daughter of Hunter. His death left Raven an orphan, as her mother had also died not too long ago. Shadow knew that he could leave Raven in the care of the older females, but this did not sit right with him. She was his niece. He was her only relative. How could he fight with honour, yet neglect to be honourable when it came to his own blood? No, he couldn't let that happen. Shadow realised that although he did not have a mate, he might soon become a father. He frowned and wondered what the rest of the Light Bearers would say about that. He was going to add a youngling to the outpost. Surely, that was more shocking than the whole mating business, he reasoned.

Shadow looked up as the sun cast its first rays over the valley and then drew a deep breath as he recalled his previous thoughts of just days ago. He smiled when he realised that despite everything – repentance, forgiveness, peace and love had managed to tip the scale back again. And that was more than enough. He could manage with such gifts. A new day had dawned and with it came the promise of a new beginning. Later he would work things out; but for now, he would share in the joy with his brethren.

Chapter 25

Boforic sat back, rubbed his tummy and a loud burp escaped from his mouth. He chuckled and said, "Aye, twas a good meal."

Looking down into the faces of his three companions, he felt pride swell in his chest. They looked so pleased. He realised then that the seed he had planted in their hearts would soon sprout and deliver another generation of great, honourable keepers. It had been a good idea to travel with them. Seeing them so inspired made him realise that his own purpose as a law keeper was not lost.

For many years he had travelled to various parts of the land, to sign treaties, enforce the law and threaten different races to keep their vows. It was not always a nice job, but when the rare opportunity presented it, he would inspire and give revelations of the importance of the law. This in return fulfilled him. He was surprised by Airon's small hand tugging on him.

"Aye lad?"

Airon's bright eyes were shiny like two blue sapphires. "Boforic, did they ever find the thief?"

Boforic laughed with sheer pleasure. "Aye, a black rat."

"A black rat!" Dusty exclaimed with a frown. "But you told us that Aire and Shadow were convinced that it could not have been an animal because of the pact with the zoionlings?" he added in disbelief.

Airon and Drizzle nodded in agreement. Boforic pulled on his long beard. "Aye, I did tell ye that. Ye see the black rat and his family were foreigners in these lands. They came through the dark mountain tunnels. They did nay ken about the pact," he explained as he pointed towards the entrance that led into the cave.

Drizzle was not convinced. "What about the guards? How did the rat get into the storerooms without being seen," he inquired, narrowing his eyes in suspicion. Boforic smiled and revealed his broken teeth.

"Och, ye lads are doubting. Why canna ye just believe what I tell ye?"

Drizzle didn't seem the least bit offended and increased his narrow-eyed stare, to the point where Boforic became uncomfortable. *The young male has a gift for extracting information with only a stare*, he observed with delight.

"Ye see, tis black rat was a clever rat. He found the secret tunnel that lead to the storeroom. No one saw him enter or leave, because he used the secret entrances in and out of the chambers."

"Ah," came the simultaneous reply from the three young males. It all made sense now.

"Aye, they only found out much later, when one of the females caught him doing so," Boforic added, nodding his head to emphasise the revelation.

Dusty shook his head. "Can you believe it? A rat! Our race nearly became extinct because of a rat."

"Who also happened to be a clever thief," Drizzle added dryly. Airon smiled again and Boforic wondered again how the serious Aire got along with his cheerful son. He had to smother a chuckle when the young male asked, "What did they do with the rat? Did they skin it?"

Boforic lifted his eyebrows in surprise, as he looked at the young male. *Mayhap the young lad is nay so innocent after all*, he thought. "Yer keepers lad, ye don't skin animals. Nay, they did what good keepers do. They welcomed him and his family, and the zoionlings formed a pact with his kind."

Dusty threw his hands up in disbelief and Boforic could almost see a younger Muddy before him.

"All the battles, all that sorrow and the thief was welcomed?"

Boforic scowled at him and then his gazed moved over the other two friends as well. "Ye ken lads; I understand that yer young and ye would like some battles and adventure. But I was hoping that ye learned something from the tale. Life is precious. Ye, as keepers should know tis," he reprimanded, the gloomy expression on his face reflecting his feelings about death.

The three young males fiddled uncomfortably, not knowing how to hide their guilt. A voice from behind startled them. "It seems that my son and his two friends are in need of some tough training," Aire's voice rumbled.

"Dad," Airon exclaimed, jumping up to greet his father.

Aire smiled and ruffled his son's hair and then he turned to the dwarf and greeted him in the old way of the warriors, awkward as it was with their difference in size. A clapping of hands drew their attention and then they saw Muddy, Raine and Shadow approaching from the entrance of the big hall. It was a joyful reunion as fathers met sons and an old friend they had not seen in years.

Raine stood with his arm rested on Drizzle's shoulder, when he spoke. "We need to go to the Sacred Chamber. The elders, your mothers and the rest of the keepers are waiting."

Drizzle looked at his dad and frowned. "But we are not late, are we? Why are they waiting for us?"

Raine flashed his deep dimples and his eyes found those of his friends. "Well son, as you know by now, after the ceremony that will honour the renewal of the treaty, our young, almost mature keepers, are called upon to continue our way of life. You three are old enough now to choose if you want to remain at our keep in the southern outpost or if you want to leave and tend to your own outpost. You would, of course, be joined by three more keepers to complete the representation of all tribes. Before this, you will first need to train together to prepare yourselves."

The three young males beamed with excitement.

"But are we ready, dad?" asked Airon enthusiastically, as he looked into his father's eyes.

"Yes, you are, son." Aire replied proudly.

Muddy cleared his throat. "You will have to train as a unit though," he added, his eyes holding those of Dusty. Obviously, he had not forgotten his son's previous remark about the lack of revenge the keepers had shown to the black rat. The young males were in dire need of more discipline and respect.

Shadow rubbed his hands together in excitement. "Well, that settles it. We will start with training at sunrise. I will inform Raven," he added cheerfully as he strolled away towards the entry of the Sacred Chamber.

The eyes of the young males grew big.

"Raven will train with us?" Dusty asked uncertainly, swallowing hard at the lump in his throat.

"Yes son, it is only fitting that the young of the Light Bearers continue our legacy," Muddy replied with a knowing smile.

"Aye, the lass may teach ye stubborn lads a few things," Boforic added and a rumble of laughter erupted from his chest.

Dusty lowered his head as he whispered to his friends. "Drizzle, your dad did say three more would join us to complete the team. How did I miss that one? Of course, the fourth one amongst us would be Raven," he murmured.

"I suppose we will just have to make friends then," Drizzle announced.

"We doona have much of a choice, lads," Airon joked, impersonating the dwarf. They quickly smothered their snickering when Boforic snarled at them.

"Enough jesting, lads. Let's get moving. Ye still have to announce yer choice to everyone," the old dwarf declared.

Aire directed them toward the Sacred Chamber and the young males had big smiles. They were so ready for this. Whether they would actually want to leave their home once the training was complete would be another issue to deal with, when the time called for it. For now, they were happy to be with their families and the prospect of training to become great warriors like their parents was more than appealing to them. Finally, they had their own quest to look forward to.

The young males were astonished at the large cave chamber. It was filled with every member of their race, as they all gathered in a bid to renew the treaty that was signed so long ago. Airon didn't know where to look, as the Sacred Chamber was breathtaking with its lovely gemstones and the reflective colours in the rock pools. Some keepers were sitting in the pools, others were seated high up on rocks and some were standing against the surrounding walls.

Dusty's eyes found the back wall, known as the sacred wall of scrolls. His mouth dropped open at the sight of it. It looked like a throne of jewels. He knew that all their recorded history lay hidden behind the various gemstones. The fine markings on the stones indicated which scroll was hidden inside.

"Is it in there?" Dusty whispered to his friends, as he indicated with his eyes towards the wall. Drizzle shook his head slowly, but it was Airon who cleared the confusion.

"I heard my dad say that the treaty is not kept amongst them. This special scroll is kept in the palace of the Ancient One and every two decades, a law keeper fetches it and brings it to our race, who then renew the vows and sign the scroll again," he explained.

Dusty's eyes lit up in understanding as a revelation dawned on him.

"This means that Boforic had the treaty all along. He tricked us. He said it was in the secret place!" Dusty looked confused as his scrutinising gaze rested upon Airon.

"You knew all along then?"

Airon shook his head in denial.

"No, I once overheard my dad telling someone. I didn't say I understood. Now I do," he said with a wide grin.

"But you knew Boforic was lying. Why did you not say anything?" Drizzle asked.

Airon donned his charming smile again. "Adventure lads, adventure!" he teased.

They erupted in laughter, realising that Airon orchestrated their adventure from the beginning. He was his father's son, after all. "Shh," came a reprimand from Raine.

The elders were seated around the huge rock table which Boforic had told them about. The dwarf stepped forward and looked at the gathered body before him. He dug into his bag and retrieved the scroll. Airon blinked at Dusty and smiled.

"Keepers of Equilibria, tis an honour to be here tonight. As you ken, Boforic has travelled far to bring tis scroll to ye. Aye, the Ancient One himself guarded it. Tis should tell ye how important it is to him, but ye ken how important it is to ye also."

He slowly broke the golden seal that protected it and then he carefully unrolled it. He narrowed his eyes as he strained to read from the document and then he shifted around, to find a position to shine more light onto it. When he finally seemed satisfied, he began to read.

"We, the tribes of Equilibria, pledge our lives, to the forest and every living thing in it. We vow never to kill another keeper and accept that the punishment for such a crime is death. We understand that we cannot survive without each other and therefore, we promise to respect all tribes. We vow to function together as one and serve

each other in honour, so that peace may always be amongst us. From this day forward, we are no longer divided as airlings, aqualings, earthlings, zoionlings, woodlings or plantlings. We are now only keepers. We declare ourselves as one body, with one purpose, for the benefit of all."

The old dwarf smiled and rubbed his eyes. When he realised that he was getting emotional before the entire keeper race, he quickly cleared his throat and said, "Aye, tis something in me eye."

Boforic held the scroll up for all to see and then said, "Ye have all made a mark with yer own blood on it. Today ye must do so again, but tis time, yer young must also put their own marks on it. Before ye get to it, ye must tell them the old tale that they ken why they have to do so."

The commanders and elders took turns as they educated the handful of young keepers about the past that had shaped them to become a great race. From time to time, a Light Bearer would give accounts of what happened. When the tale was finally finished, the young joined in the pledge and gave their marks. The parents of the young keepers asked them to decide on what journey they would like to embark. Some chose to remain in the city of Par, while others chose to remain at the dwellings where they had been raised. There was of course the handful of those, who were brave enough, who chose to train and become warriors. They would eventually defend and be in charge of their own outpost. Amongst them were the proud sons of the Light Bearers, and one very potent daughter too. Dusty's eyes found those of the dark beauty Raven and he smiled at her. To his surprise, she didn't bite him; instead, she smiled right back at him.

In the big hall of the palace, the celebratory feast was glorious. Airon, Dusty and Drizzle looked at Boforic, who returned his own thankful stare. A moment of admiration passed between them. The dwarf was glad that the young males stirred his passion again. The three young males could not contain their joy. They were happy to know that the recent tale that was told did not come close to the one that they already heard. The one they knew about had inspired them, not just to be good, but to be exceptional keepers.

It was strange how their innocent lives changed overnight and that, at the break of dawn, they would embark on a new journey – one that would lead them to become warriors, united in purpose and strength, just like their parents were. Who knows, "mayhap" as the old dwarf would say, they too would one day be known as honourable warriors and become as great as the Light Bearers. Did not the Light Bearers also find themselves in the midst of change overnight and was it not their example of unity and the power it yields that saved all keepers and Equilibria? Their future may be unknown, but one thing was certain, they would hold on to the truth that was engraved onto their hearts. They were keepers, not just united together as one, but dependent upon one another for survival. This lesson of the past would be their light, and honour would be their guide.

Noreen Arangies

Namibian author Noreen Arangies writes books for children and young teenagers. She uses creative and descriptive writing to educate young developing minds. Viewing children as humanity's future and main responsibility, she focuses on moral values, choices and accountability, while keeping her stories captivating and entertaining. As a young girl, she found an outlet in writing down her thoughts and this practise has developed into a cherished platform for ideas and creativity. Having a keen imaginative intellect, Noreen was inspired to write children's books after the birth of her son. She began her career in children's literature with *The Most Important Book*, published by Wordweaver Publishing House 2012. Targeted at primary school readers, the book won a gold award at the Namibian Children's Book Forum Awards Ceremony, in October 2012.